F R I D A Y

MICHEL TOURNIER

· · · · · · · · · · · · · · · · ·

FRIDAY

TRANSLATED FROM THE FRENCH
BY NORMAN DENNY

PANTHEON BOOKS, NEW YORK

Library of Congress Cataloging in Publication Data
Tournier, Michel.
Friday.
Translation of: Vendredi.
I. Denny, Norman, 1901– II. Title.
PQ2680.083V413   1985   843'.914   84-22784
ISBN 0-394-72880-7

Manufactured in the United States of American

First Pantheon Paperback Edition

There is always another island.

JEAN GUÉHENNO

PROLOGUE

With the precision of a lead line the lantern hanging from the cabin roof measured by the extent of its swing the roll of the brig Virginia in a sea that was growing steadily worse. Captain Pieter Van Deyssel bent forward over his stomach to place the tarot pack on the table in front of Robinson.

"Cut and turn up the top card," he said.

He lay back in his chair and puffed smoke from his china-bowled pipe.

"So it is the Demiurge," he said. "One of the three major fundamental Arcana. The picture shows a tumbler standing at a bench scattered with miscellaneous objects. This means that in you there is an organizer, one who does battle with a world in disorder which he seeks to master by whatever means come to his hand. He appears to succeed, but we must not forget that the Demiurge is also an acrobat: his work is an illusion and his order illusory. Alas, he is unaware of this. Skepticism is not his strength."

A heavy thud shook the ship and the lantern made an angle of forty-five degrees with the roof. The Virginia had suddenly swung so that she lay almost across the wind, and a wave had crashed with a sound like cannon fire onto the deck. Robinson turned up the next card. It depicted, smeared

with splashes of grease, a crowned and sceptered figure standing upright in a chariot drawn by two horses.

"Mars," said the captain. "The little Demiurge has achieved
a seeming victory over Nature. He has triumphed by force
of will and imposed an order which is in his own image."

Hunched like a Buddha in his chair, Van Deyssel gazed
at Robinson with eyes twinkling with malice.

"An order in your own image," he repeated thoughtfully.
"Nothing so gratifies a man's soul as his belief that he has
the power to impose his will without restriction. Robinson
the king . . . You are twenty-two. You have deserted—that
is to say, you have left behind in York—a young wife and
two children, to seek your fortune in the New World, like
so many of your compatriots. Later they are to join you—if
God permits. Your close-cropped hair and square, russet
beard, your clear-eyed, steady gaze, in which there is a hint
of something narrow and rigid, your attire, whose sobriety
is near to affectation—all this puts you in the happy category
of those who have never had doubts. You are pious, parsimonious, and pure. The kingdom over which you will preside
will be like one of those great tidy cupboards where the
women of our country keep their piles of immaculate linen
scented with lavender. You must not resent these remarks.
You need not blush. What I am saying would be mortifying
only if you were twenty years older. The truth is that you
have everything to learn. Stop blushing and turn up another
card. . . . What did I tell you? That is the Hermit. The
warrior has become conscious of his solitude. He has with-
drawn into the depths of a cave to seek the wellspring of his
life. But in doing so, in burying himself in the bosom of the
earth and exploring to the depths of himself, he has become
another man. If ever he emerges from his retreat he will

find that his monolithic soul has been intimately fissured. Draw another card."

Robinson hesitated. This bulky Dutch Silenus, lapped in a luxuriating materialism, was saying things with decidedly uncomfortable undertones. Since taking passage in the Virginia at Lima, Robinson had contrived to avoid any close contact with the devilish man, being soon put off by his dismaying perspicacity and cynical Epicureanism. It was due to this storm that he found himself in some sort a prisoner in the captain's cabin, it being the only place in the ship where any shred of comfort remained; and Van Deyssel seemed resolved to make the most of the chance of amusing himself at the expense of his simple-minded passenger. When Robinson refused a drink he had produced the tarot pack, and now—while the storm thundered in Robinson's ears like the din of a witches' Sabbath accompanying the unholy game in which he was obliged to take part—he was richly indulging his gift of prophecy.

"Well, here's something to bring the Hermit out of his hole! Venus, no less, rises from the waters and takes her first steps on your drab earth. May I have another card? Aha, Sagittarius, the sixth Mystery. Venus, become a winged angel, shoots arrows at the sun. Another, please. Oh, dear! You have turned up the twenty-first Mystery, that of Chaos! The Beast of the Earth is in conflict with a monster of flame. The man you see, caught between opposed forces, is a clown recognizable by his cap and bells—or at least he will become one. Another card. Well, this was to be expected. It is Saturn, the twelfth Mystery, depicted as a hanged man. But what is significant about the figure is that, as you see, he is hanging by his feet. You are head down, my poor Crusoe. Another card quickly! It is the Twins, the fifteenth Mystery.

I was wondering what would be the next avatar of our
Venus transformed into an archer. She has become your twin
brother. The Twins are depicted attached by the neck to the
feet of the bisexual angel. Take particular note of that!"
Robinson's thoughts were wandering. Yet the groaning of
the ship's hull under the battering of the waves was not causing him undue alarm, any more than the reeling flight of
the scatter of stars visible through the skylight above the
captain's head. The Virginia, an unhandy ship in light airs,
was at her sturdy best in heavy weather. With her stubby,
unraked masts and short, beamy hull of 250 tons she looked
more like a floating washpot than a greyhound of the seas,
and her lack of speed was a subject for jesting in every
port she tied up in; but her crew could sleep soundly through
the roughest gale, and the nearness of the shore was no cause
for concern. To this might be added the temperament of her
skipper, who was not the man to affront winds and tides
or run undue risks for the sake of holding his course.

In the early evening of September 29, 1759, when the
ship was in the 32nd parallel of the southern latitude, the
glass had fallen sharply while St. Elmo's fire twinkled at the
ends of masts and spars, heralding a storm of exceptional
violence. The southern skyline toward which the brig was
sluggishly heading was so black that when the first drops of
spray fell on deck Robinson was surprised to find them
colorless. A sulfurous darkness enveloped the ship while a
wind of gale force blew up, coming approximately from the
northwest, but gusting and veering through five or six points
of the compass. The easygoing Virginia had been forced to
battle as best she might with a long, deep swell that buried
her bows as she emerged from every trough; but she had
continued on course with a sturdiness that brought a tear to

*the sardonic eye of Van Deyssel. However, after two hours,
a sound like an explosion had brought him running on deck
to find that his mizzen had burst like a balloon and was
now no more than a few shreds of tattered canvas. With
honor satisfied, and feeling that he need defy the elements
no longer, he had put the ship about and ordered the helms-
man to hold her before the wind. It was as though the storm
had acknowledged this act of surrender. Since then the Virginia had sailed without undue buffeting through a tempes-
tuous sea whose furies seemed suddenly to have lost interest
in her. Having seen to it that she was fully battened down,
Van Deyssel had sent the rest of the crew below, except
for a lookout and the ship's dog, Tenn, who remained on
the poop. He then installed himself in his cabin with all the
consolations of Dutch philosophy—a flask of Hollands, a
cheese flavored with caraway seed, slices of pumpernickel,
a teapot heavy as a curbstone, a pipe, and a tobacco jar. Ten
days earlier a green line on the port horizon had told them
that the ship, having entered the Tropic of Capricorn, was
passing the Desventurado Islands. Heading south, she should
on the following day have entered the waters of the Islands
of Fernández; but the storm was driving her eastward toward
the coast of Chile, from which she was still one hundred
and seventy sea miles distant, with no intervening island or
reef, according to the chart. There was therefore no cause
for alarm.*

*The captain, whose voice had been drowned for some
moments by the tumult, now resumed his discourse:*

*"We again find the Twins in the nineteenth major Mystery,
the Arcanum of the Lion. Two children hold hands in front
of a wall symbolizing the City of the Sun. The Sun-god
fills all the upper part of the picture, which is dedicated to*

him. In the City of the Sun, set between Time and Eternity, between Life and Death, the inhabitants are clothed with childlike innocence, having attained to solar sexuality, which is not merely androgynous but circular. *A snake biting its tail is the symbol of that self-enclosed eroticism, in which there is no leak or flaw. It is the zenith of human perfectibility, infinitely difficult to achieve, more difficult still to sustain. It seems that you are destined to rise even to these heights, or so the Egyptian tarot cards say. My compliments, young sir." Rising on his cushions, the captain made Robinson a little bow of mingled irony and deference. "But may I have yet another card? Ah, it is Capricorn, the door which is the soul's way out—that is to say, death. The fateful tale is told clearly enough by the skeleton mowing a meadow planted with hands, feet, and heads. Flung down from the heights of the City of the Sun, you are in grave danger of death. I long to see the card which follows, and I dread it. If it is a weak symbol your story is done. . . ."*

Robinson was now straining his ears for something else. Had he not heard, mingled with the grand cacophony of wind and sea, the sound of a human voice on deck, and the barking of a dog? It was hard to tell, and perhaps he was too preoccupied with the thought of the lookout man, exposed to all the fury of that hellish storm. The man was so securely roped to a stanchion that he might have had difficulty in releasing himself to give the alarm, or have feared to do so. But would his voice have been heard amid the tumult? Had he not cried out just now?

"Jupiter!" exclaimed the captain. "Jove! Robinson, you are saved, but at the very last moment! You were falling like a plummet, and the great god has come most expeditiously to your aid. Here he is, in the guise of a golden child,

issue of the entrails of the earth, like a nugget from a mine, restoring to you the keys of the City of the Sun."

Jove . . . Was not that the word Robinson had heard amid the roar of the tempest? Jove . . . But then he realized that it must have been a sound resembling it, the syllable "ho." That was what the man on deck had shouted, what any lookout must have shouted, catching a brief, terrifying glimpse of an unknown, uncharted coastline—"Land-ho!"

"All this may seem to you a meaningless farrago," resumed Van Deyssel. "But it is a part of the wisdom of the tarot cards that they do not predict our future in precise terms. Think of the dismay if they did! They do no more than afford us, at the best, an intimation. My brief lecture is in some sort a coded message, and the key to the cipher is your future itself. Each forthcoming event in your life will in its occurrence reveal the truth of one or other of my predictions. Prophecy of this kind is not so illusory as it may at first appear."

He drew thoughtfully at the curved mouthpiece of his long-stemmed Alsatian pipe. It had gone out. Getting a pen-knife out of his pocket, he scraped the dottle from the china bowl into the scallop-shell which served him as an ash tray. Robinson, still intently listening, heard no more human sounds amid the tempest. The captain opened his big tobacco jar by means of the leather tab fixed to its tight-fitting wooden lid, and carefully inserted the pipe in a trough scooped in the tobacco which nearly filled the jar.

"Thus it is secured against shocks," he explained, "besides being impregnated with the honeyed scent of Amsterdamer." Then, become suddenly motionless, he looked hard at Robinson. "Crusoe," he said sternly, "take heed of what I say. Beware of purity. It is the acid of the soul."

At this moment the lantern, swinging with a sudden wildness on its chain, smashed against the cabin roof, and at the same time the captain was flung head foremost across the table. Plunged into a sudden, shuddering darkness, Robinson tried to feel his way to the door. He found none, but presently a violent blast of air told him that he was in the alleyway outside the cabin. He stood trembling, afflicted in his entire body by the terrifying immobility that had succeeded the plunging movement of the ship. Up on deck, by the tragic light of a full moon, he saw a party of sailors attempting to hoist a lifeboat on its davits. He started to go toward them, and as he did so the planks were swept out from under his feet. A blow struck the port side of the vessel that was like the battering of a thousand rams. An instant later a black wall of water fell with a crash upon the deck, sweeping it from end to end and carrying everything away, men and gear alike.

FRIDAY

CHAPTER ONE

A wave curled and running up the wet shore licked Robinson's toes as he lay face down on the sand. Still only half conscious, he drew in his legs and crawled a few yards higher up the beach. Then he rolled over on his back. Black and white gulls wheeled screeching in a limpid sky where only a wisp of white, drifting eastward, remained to tell of yesterday's storm. Robinson tried to sit up and as he did so felt a sharp pain in his left shoulder. The shore was littered with gutted fish, shattered shellfish, and piles of brownish weed, such as grows only in a certain depth of water. North and east the skyline was open sea, but to the west it was broken by a rocky promontory which seemed to continue under water in a series of reefs. It was here, some two cable lengths away, that the ridiculous and pathetic shape of the *Virginia* rested, propped amid the sharp outcroppings, her broken masts and tangled shrouds a mute proclamation of disaster.

When the storm had burst upon her the ship must have been lying to the northeast of the Juan Fernández archipelago, and not due north of it as Van Deyssel had supposed. Running before the wind, she must have been driven down on to the outer reefs of the island of Más a Tierra instead of heading into the hundred and seventy miles of open sea which separated that island from the Chilean coast. This at any rate was the theory least unfavorable for Robinson, since Más a Tierra, described by William Dampier, was populated by people of Spanish extraction, rather thinly scattered, it was true, amid the forests and grasslands of its sixty-odd square miles. But it was also possible that the captain had made no mistake in his reckoning, and that the *Virginia* had run aground on an uncharted island somewhere between Juan Fernández and the American continent. However that might be, he must set about looking for other survivors from the wreck, and for inhabitants of the island, if such there were.

Robinson got to his feet and walked a few paces. No bones were broken, but his left shoulder was badly bruised. Fearing the intensity of the sun, which was high in the sky, he fashioned a conical hat for himself out of a frond of the ferns which grew thickly between the beach and the edge of the forest, and, picking up a fallen branch to serve him as a walking stick, he entered the thorny undergrowth at the foot of the volcanic upland, from the crest of which he hoped to be able to survey the land.

Gradually the forest grew denser. Thorny shrubs gave way to scented laurels, red cedar, and pine. The trunks of dead and rotting trees lay in such confusion that at times he found himself walking through tunnels of vegetation and at other times several yards above ground level, as though on a natural footbridge. The tangle of creepers and hanging branches enclosed him like a vast net, and in the heavy silence of the forest the noise of his progress exploded in frightening echoes. Not only did he come upon no trace of human habitation, but even animals seemed absent from the leafy cathedrals that stretched before him. At first, approaching a motionless shape some thirty yards away which might have been that of a sheep or large goat, he supposed it to be a tree stump, hardly any stranger than others he had passed. But as he drew near he found that this object in the green gloom was indeed some sort of wild goat, with very long hair. Head raised and ears cocked, it stood in rocklike immobility, watching his approach, and he felt a tremor of superstitious terror at the thought that he must either walk past the weird creature or turn back. Discarding his stick, which was too light, he picked up a black, knotted cudgel of wood, strong enough to break the goat's impetus if it charged.

He stopped two paces away from it. Out of the mass of hair a single green eye with a dark oval pupil was staring at him. Robinson recalled that, owing to the wide set of their eyes, the majority of quadrupeds can look at things only in a one-eyed fashion, and that a charging bull cannot see the adversary it is charging. A strange sound issued from the hairy statue obstructing his path, like a deep belly chuckle. With fear exacerbating his state of extreme fatigue, Robinson was overtaken by a violent fit of anger. Raising his cudgel, he brought it down with all his strength between the goat's horns. There was a crunching sound, the animal sank on its knees and then rolled over on its side. It was the first living creature Robinson had encountered on the island, and he had killed it.

After several hours' climb he came to the foot of a rocky mass, at the base of which the black mouth of a cave opened up. He went inside and found it to be enormous, so deep and vast that for the present he could not explore it. He left it and clambered to the top of the great pile of rock, which seemed to be the highest point of the surrounding terrain. Reaching the summit, he found that indeed he could see the whole circle of the horizon—and the sea was everywhere. He was on an island much smaller than Más a Tierra, which gave no sign of human habitation. He now understood the goat's strange behavior. The creature had never before set eyes on a human being: sheer curiosity had kept it rooted to the spot. Robinson was too exhausted to measure the full extent of his misfortune. "Since it isn't Más a Tierra," he reflected simply, "then it is the Island of Desolation," summing up his own situation with this impromptu baptism. But the sun was now sinking and he was conscious of a queasy emptiness in his stomach. Total despair presupposes the minimum of relief. Exploring the mountaintop, he found a kind of wild banana, smaller and sweeter than those of California. He dined on these, cutting them up with his clasp knife. Then he lay down in the shadow of a boulder, and fell into a dreamless sleep.

A huge cedar that had taken root near the approach to the cave rose high above the mound of rock like the tutelary genius of the island. When Robinson awoke its branches were stirring in a light breeze from the northwest as though in a gesture of consolation. Its vegetable presence was comforting and might have given Robinson a foretaste of what the island could do for him, had his thoughts not been so wholly concentrated on the sea. Since this place was not Más a Tierra, it could only be an island unknown to the map makers, lying somewhere between the Juan Fernández archipelago to the west and the Chilean coast to the east. Its distance from either was impossible to determine, but both must certainly be beyond the reach of a single man in a raft or improvised canoe. Moreover, if the island was unknown, this must mean that it was off the regular sailing routes.

While he reached this melancholy conclusion Robinson was studying the physical characteristics of the island. Its entire western half seemed to be covered by the dense coat of tropical forest, ending abruptly in sheer cliffs overhanging the sea. But on its eastern side there was an expanse of well-watered meadowland which turned to marsh as it approached a low-lying shore broken by lagoons. Only on the northern coast of the island did there seem to be a place where a boat could put in. This was a wide, sandy bay, bounded at its eastern end by white-shining dunes, and at the west by the reefs where the hull of the *Virginia* was to be seen, her rounded belly wedged in the rocks.

When finally he began to walk back down the hillside toward the beach he had left the day before, Robinson had already undergone a change. The fact of having understood and measured the solitude to which he was doomed, perhaps for a very long time, had sobered him and brought on a mood of heavy melancholy. He had forgotten all about the slaughtered goat until he came upon it on his path. It was a relief to find his cudgel lying where he had let it fall, a few yards away, because half a dozen vultures, their heads sunk between their shoulders, were watching his approach with small, pink eyes. The goat lay gutted on the stones, and the featherless, scarlet crops bulging through the plumage of the carrion birds showed that the feast was well begun.

Robinson advanced, brandishing his cudgel. The birds dispersed, running ponderously on their twisted feet, and one by one rising laboriously into the air. One of them turned and as it flew past released a green dropping which splashed on a tree trunk near Robinson. But they had done their work well. Only the goat's entrails and genitals had disappeared;

the rest would probably not have been edible by them except after days of baking in the sun. Robinson slung the body over his shoulders and went on down the path.

Back on the shore he cut off a hindquarter and roasted it, hanging it from a tripod of sticks tied together over a fire of eucalyptus twigs. The crackle of the flames consoled him more than the tough, musky-tasting meat, which he chewed with his eyes on the horizon. He resolved to keep the fire going permanently, as much for his spiritual comfort as to save the flint and steel he had found in his pocket, or as a signal to possible rescuers. In any case, nothing was more likely to attract the notice of a passing vessel than the wrecked hull of the *Virginia*, still upright amid the rocks with its shattered masts and hanging shrouds, a melancholy sight but certain to arouse the interest of any seafarer. Robinson thought of the store of arms and provisions on board, which he must try to bring ashore before another storm broke her up for good. If his stay on the island was to be a long one, his survival would depend on this legacy bequeathed him by shipmates whom he must now presume to be dead. The wise course would have been to start immediately on the salvage operations, which presented great difficulties to a man working singlehanded. However, he did not do so, telling himself that by lightening the vessel he would render her more vulnerable to any puff of wind and thus endanger his own best chance of getting away. The truth was that he felt an overwhelming reluctance to undertake any kind of work which would suggest that he was settling down on the island. Not only did he cling to the belief that his stay would be short, but he had a superstitious feeling that in making any attempt to organize his life here he would be dismissing the hope of an early rescue. With his back turned obstinately to the land, he kept his eyes fixed on the rolling, metallic surface of the sea, from which, surely, help would soon come.

During the days that followed he busied himself with every contrivance he could imagine for signaling his presence. Next to his permanent fire on the beach he collected a great pile of fagots and dried seaweed to be converted into a signal beacon if a sail showed on the horizon. Then he thought of setting up a mast with a cross-pole attached to the top, its longer end reaching to the ground. When the time came he would fix a lighted torch to the lower end and, pulling on the other with a rope of lianas, raise it high in the air. But he gave up this idea when, on the cliffs overlooking the western end of the bay, he found a dead eucalyptus tree of great height, its hollow trunk forming a natural chimney. By surrounding it with kindling he could rapidly transform the whole tree into a flaming torch visible for leagues around. He did not set up signals which might have been sighted when he was elsewhere, because he had no intention of leaving that stretch of shore, where at any moment, in an hour or two, or at the latest tomorrow or the day after, a ship would come sailing into the bay.

He gave no thought to his food, simply eating anything that came to hand—shellfish, coconuts, roots and berries, birds' eggs, and turtle eggs. On the third day he dragged the remains of the goat some distance away because it was beginning to stink intolerably. But afterward he regretted doing this since it drew the attention of the vultures to himself. Wherever he went he was accompanied by a watchful escort of bleached heads and scrawny necks. The obscene creatures merely took casual evasive action when he bombarded them with sticks and stones, as though, being the servants of death, they held themselves to be immortal.

Nor did he keep any count of the passing days, relying upon his eventual rescuers to tell him how much time had elapsed since the wreck of the *Virginia*. So he never knew precisely how many days it was—or weeks or months—before his idleness and passive contemplation of the skyline began to oppress him. The vast, gently heaving expanse of the ocean, green-tinged and glittering, fascinated him so much that he began to fear he was becoming subject to hallucinations. The first of these was his tendency to forget that what lay at his feet was a liquid mass in constant motion: he began to see it as a hard, rubbery surface on which he could walk and leap if he chose. Then, his fancy wandering further still, he came to think of it as the back of some fabulous beast whose head lay beyond the horizon. And finally, it occurred to him that the island, with its rocks and trees, was itself nothing but the lid and brow of a huge, liquid, blue eye, contemplating the immensity of the heavens. This last image so obsessed him that he had to abandon his own state of passive expectation. He shook himself and decided that he must do something. For the first time the fear of madness had entered his mind. It was never again to leave him.

To do something could mean only one thing: it meant building a boat large enough to take him to the coast of Chile.

On the day he formed this resolve Robinson also realized that he must overcome his reluctance and visit the hulk of the *Virginia* in search of tools and materials useful for his purpose. With the help of lianas he lashed together a dozen

dead logs to form a crude raft, which was, however, serviceable enough in conditions of flat calm. A stout pole was all
the propulsion he needed, because at low tide the water was
shallow until it reached the rocks, by means of which he
could then maneuver. Reaching the wreck, which towered
above him, he tied up to the sternpost and then swam around
it to find a way of getting on board. There was no visible
damage to the hull, which was wedged onto a sharp reef of
low-lying rocks which were undoubtedly always submerged.
Indeed, if the crew, putting their faith in the ship, had stayed
below instead of letting themselves be washed overboard on
deck, they might all have been saved. As he hoisted himself
up with a rope hanging from one of the davits, Robinson
reflected that he might even find Van Deyssel on board,
since he had left him, injured no doubt but still alive, in the
comparative safety of his cabin. Scrambling onto the well-
deck, which was so encumbered with the tangle of broken
masts and spars, sheets, shrouds, and halyards that it was
difficult to pick one's way through it, he saw the dead body
of the lookout, still lashed to the stanchion on the foredeck,
like the victim of an execution. The poor wretch must have
been stunned by some sudden blow before he could cut himself loose, and so he had died at his post, after fruitlessly
giving the alarm.

The ship's storerooms, down below, were in similar disorder. But at least the sea had not penetrated everywhere,
and stowed away in the lockers Robinson found supplies of
ship's biscuit and salt meat, of which he ate as much as he
could manage without fresh water. There were also casks
of wine and stone flagons of gin, but his lifelong abstinence
had left him with a natural distaste for fermented liquors.

The captain's cabin was empty, but he caught sight of the

captain lying in the navigating bay. He felt a stab of joy
when, as he thought, the heavy body made a movement, as
though responding to the sound of his voice. But the bloody,
hairy mass of the captain's head was hanging limply, and
moved only when the torso was shaken by a strange shudder.
As Robinson stood in what remained of the doorway, the
bloodstained folds of the captain's jacket were thrust apart
and an enormous rat emerged, followed by two smaller ones.
Robinson turned away, reeling, to vomit on the debris that
littered the cabin floor.

He had taken no great interest in the *Virginia*'s cargo.
Although he had asked Van Deyssel about it soon after coming on board, he had not pressed the question when the
captain had replied in a coarsely jesting tone that he specialized in Dutch cheese and guano, the latter resembling the
former in its greasy texture, its yellowish color, and its smell.
So it did not greatly surprise him when, securely lashed in
the hold, he found forty kegs of black powder.

It took him several days to get this load of explosive
ashore, because he could only navigate his raft at low tide.
In the intervals he devised a covering for it, a rainproof
shelter of palm leaves held down with stones. He also
brought two cases of ship's biscuit ashore, a spyglass, two
flintlock muskets, a double-barreled pistol, two axes, a spokeshave, a hammer, a plane, a bale of oakum, and a large bale
of coarse red cloth, cheap material designed for barter with
any natives the ship might encounter. He got the big jar
of *Amsterdamer* out of the captain's cabin, and found it
hermetically sealed with the china-bowled pipe undamaged,
securely lodged in its nest of tobacco. He took ashore a load
of planks torn from the ship's decks and bulkheads, and

finally a Bible, which he found in good condition in the mate's cabin, wrapped in a piece of sailcloth.

The next day he set about building a vessel, which he hopefully christened the *Escape*.

CHAPTER TWO

The high ground at the northwest of the island fell away, in an easily negotiable slope of rubble overgrown with sparse shrubs, to a sandy creek. Overlooking this creek was a flat clearing, about an acre and a half in extent, and near it Robinson discovered, half-buried in the undergrowth, a long, straight, slender tree trunk, evidently recently fallen, dry but in excellent condition, which would serve for the keelson of the *Escape*. The small plateau had the advantage of offering a view over that part of the sea where help might appear, and the hollow eucalyptus, which Robinson intended to use as a signal beacon, was also close at hand. Accordingly, he took all his tools and materials there, having decided to make the clearing his shipyard.

Before starting work, he read several pages of the Bible aloud. Having been brought up a Quaker, the sect to which his mother belonged, he had never been a great student of Holy Writ. But his extraordinary circumstances, and the chance, as though it were the direct intervention of Providence, which had placed the Book of Books in his hands as his sole spiritual sustenance, moved him to search those ancient pages for the moral support he so greatly needed. And on the first day, he thought that he found in Chapter VI of the Book of Genesis, with its account of the Flood and the building of the Ark, a clear allusion to the vessel of salvation he was about to build.

After clearing away the bushes to give himself working space, he topped and tailed the trunk, leaving a central section which he judged to be long enough for his requirements. He lopped the branches off this section and then, using poles as levers and helped by the slight slope on which it lay, he rolled it onto the plateau, and, still using his ax, set about squaring it along its entire length.

He worked slowly and by rule of thumb, guided only by his recollection of visits paid as a child to a small shipyard on the river Ouse which specialized in fishing vessels, and later of his efforts with his brothers to build a rowing boat —an attempt which they had finally abandoned. But he now had limitless time at his disposal, and inexorable necessity drove him to his task. When discouragement came near to overwhelming him he compared his lot with that of the prisoner painfully using an improvised tool to file through the bars of his cell, or striving to scratch a hole in the wall with his fingernails, and then he felt fortunate. Moreover, having neglected to keep a calendar since the wreck, he had only the vaguest idea of the passing of time. The days flowed monotonously by, each like the last, and every morning he had the sensation of starting again on the day before.

Technical problems greatly troubled him. Those boatbuilders on the Ouse had bent the planks for the strakes around forms, with the aid of steam; but he had no means of constructing a boiler on this scale, and he could only whittle them roughly with his ax and spokeshave. The shaping of the stem- and sternposts proved so difficult that he had to finish them off with his clasp knife. He was obsessed with the fear of damaging the original tree trunk which had so providentially furnished him with a keel.

Seeing the vultures swoop over the wreck of the *Virginia*, he suffered pangs of conscience at the thought that he had left the bodies of the captain and the lookout man unburied. The horrid task of getting their bulky and rotting corpses ashore was one that he constantly postponed, and to have pushed them overboard would have been to run the risk of attracting sharks, which would then no doubt have hung about the bay hoping for further prey. It was bad enough to have attracted the attention of the vultures; now they never left him. He concluded that it would be time enough, when the rats and birds between them had stripped the bodies clean, to collect the skeletons and consign them to a decent grave. He even made a vow that he would build a chapel and say a prayer for them there every day. Since the dead were now his only companions, it was right that they should have a place of honor in his life.

In all his searches he had found no screws or nails aboard the *Virginia*, and, having no instrument for drilling holes, he could not fix the planks together by pegging. He had to use mortise and tenon, rounding the latter in a fishtail for greater strength. He even had the idea of hardening the fishtails with fire and then wetting them with sea water so they would lodge more securely in each mortise. This constantly caused the wood to split under the influence of fire or water, but he doggedly remade them, living now in a kind of somnambulistic torpor, beyond weariness or haste.

Sudden showers and trails of white on the horizon announced a change in the weather. The sky one morning, although still cloudless overhead, had taken on a metallic tinge that worried him. The limpid blue of the previous days had turned leaden and colorless. Before long a coverlet of cloud, of perfectly even density, stretched from one horizon to the other, and the first heavy raindrops beat on the timbers of the *Escape*. Robinson tried at first to ignore them, but he was soon obliged to strip off his clothes, whose sodden weight hampered his movements. After stowing these for shelter in the completed part of the hull, he stood for a moment watching the tepid water flow over his body, carrying away its accretions of earth and dirt in little muddy balls. His ginger body hair, now plastered down and glistening, was patterned by the rain's lines of force, which accentuated its animal nature. "A golden seal," he reflected with a faint smile. Then he made water, pleased to add his modest contribution to the downpour drenching the earth around him. He suddenly felt as though he were on holiday, and in a burst of high spirits he danced a few steps before running, half-blinded by the rain and whipped by the gusts of wind, to take cover under the trees.

The rain had not yet penetrated the numberless layers of foliage on which it beat down thunderously, while a heavy mist rose from the earth and was lost in the high, leafy arches. Robinson expected the rain to break through at any moment and drench him, but instead the earth beneath his feet grew increasingly spongy, although not a drop fell on his body. He understood the reason for this when he saw water running down the tree trunks along small folds in the bark that might have been gutters expressly carved for the purpose. After some hours the beams of the setting sun, breaking through a gap between the horizon and the ceiling of cloud, bathed the island in a fiery light, although the rain still fell with undiminished violence.

Robinson's mood of childlike gaiety had soon abated, together with the kind of intoxication which had kept him
working at his self-imposed task. He felt himself sinking into
a limbo of despair, naked and alone in that apocalyptic landscape, his only companions two corpses rotting in a wrecked
ship. Only later did he fully grasp the import of that experience of nakedness, which he had undergone for the first
time. It was true that neither the temperature nor any consideration of modesty required him to go about dressed in a
civilized manner. Sheer habit had caused him to do so, and
now in his despair he began to appreciate the value of that
armor of wool and linen with which human society had
hitherto protected him. Nakedness is a luxury in which a
man may indulge himself without danger only when he is
warmly surrounded by his fellow man. For Robinson, while
his soul had not yet undergone any change, it was a trial
of desperate temerity. Stripped of its threadbare garments
—worn, tattered, and sullied, but the fruit of civilized millennia, and impregnated with human associations—his vulnerable
body was at the mercy of every hostile element. The wind,
the thorned shrubs, the rocks, and the pitiless light assailed
and tormented their defenseless prey. Robinson felt that he
was doomed to perish. Had human creature ever been subjected to so harsh an ordeal? For the first time since the
wreck, words of revolt against the decrees of Providence
rose to his lips. "O Lord," he murmured, "if Thou hast not
turned Thy face wholly away from Thy servant, if Thou
dost not desire him soon to succumb beneath the weight of
the desolation Thou hast inflicted upon him, then must Thou
show Thyself! Give me a sign that I may know that Thy
Presence is still near me!" Tight-lipped, he waited, like the
first man under the Tree of Knowledge when the earth was

still soft and damp after the receding of the waters. And then, though the rain beat yet more heavily on the leaves and it seemed that all things must dissolve in the mist rising from the earth, he saw taking shape on the horizon a rainbow greater and more dazzling than Nature alone could have contrived. More than a rainbow, it was an almost perfect halo, with only its lowest segment buried in the waves, radiating the seven colors of the spectrum with astonishing brilliance.

The downpour ceased as suddenly as it had begun, and with his clothes Robinson regained his sense of the purpose and urgency of his task. He had soon recovered from that brief but instructive moment of despair.

He was in the act of coupling a side member into its precisely shaped socket, bearing down on it with all his weight, when he had a feeling that he was being watched. Looking around, he met the gaze of Tenn, the *Virginia*'s dog, a setter of doubtful breeding but warmly affectionate disposition. It had stopped a few yards away and was observing him with ears cocked and one forepaw raised. A great happiness flooded through Robinson. After all, he was not the only survivor of the wreck! He walked toward the animal, speaking its name. Tenn was one of those dogs who have an absolute need of human companionship, the sound of a human voice, and the touch of a human hand. It was strange, then, that instead of running to greet Robinson with his tail wagging he should have backed away, furiously growling, with teeth bared. He turned abruptly and bolted into the wood.

Despite his disappointment, Robinson derived a pleasure from this encounter that buoyed him up during the next few days. Moreover, Tenn's curious behavior diverted his mind from the problems of the *Escape* by giving him something else to think about. Did it mean that the terror and ordeal of the shipwreck had driven the poor beast mad? Or was he so disconsolate at the captain's death that he could not endure the presence of any other man? But another thought occurred to Robinson that filled him with alarm. Perhaps they had been so long on the island that the dog had simply reverted to its natural, wild state. How long was it since the shipwreck? How many days, weeks, months, even years, had passed? He was assailed with a kind of dizziness when he asked the question, as though he had dropped a stone into a well and were listening in vain for it to reach the bottom. He resolved henceforth to make a notch on a tree trunk for every day that passed, with a cross to mark every thirtieth day. Then he forgot the matter and went back to work on the *Escape*.

She slowly took shape, that of a beamy straight-stemmed craft, rather heavy and with very little sheer, about eighteen feet on the water line. He could do with nothing less if he were to have a reasonable hope of making the coast of Chile. She was to have one mast and a single spar carrying a large loose-footed sail, easily handled by a single man and designed to make the most of the beam wind he expected to meet on his easterly course. The mast was to pass through the forward decking and be stepped solidly in the keel. Before proceeding to lay the deck, he ran his hand for the last time over the smooth and closely joined interior surface of the boat's sides, thinking happily of the beads of moisture that must appear when she first took the water. She would need to float for a day or two before her timbers swelled enough to make her watertight. The deck planking alone, to be laid across the thwarts securing the sides of the hull, had cost him several weeks of arduous toil. But a decked forepeak or cuddy was indispensable for the housing of his provisions. Even though, if his hazy estimate was correct and the Chilean coast was less than two hundred miles distant, he might hope in favorable conditions to reach it in a couple of days, he must make ample allowance for miscalculation and the vagaries of wind and tide.

Throughout his work he had been handicapped by the lack of a saw, having failed to find one in his search of the *Virginia*. It was a tool which he had no means of improvising, and it would have spared him months of labor with ax and knife. So much did the thought of this obsess him that one morning, hearing a sound which might have been that of a man sawing, he thought he must be the victim of a hallucination. Now and then there was an interval, as though the worker had paused to rest, and then, with monotonous regularity, the sound began again. Robinson crept out of the cranny in the rocks where he was accustomed to sleep and advanced cautiously toward it, steeling himself against the possible shock of encountering another human being. He found the workman to be a giant crab using one pincer to saw the end off a coconut which it held with its other claw. Up in the coconut palm, some twenty feet above ground, another crab was detaching the nuts at their stem and letting them fall to the ground. The two creatures seemed quite unperturbed by his arrival, and went on quietly with their business.

The sight of them was intensely repugnant to Robinson. He walked on to his clearing, more convinced than ever that this place was wholly alien and hostile, and that his boat, whose large, comforting silhouette could be glimpsed through the bushes, was his only link with life.

Having no varnish or tar for calking, he made a kind of resinous dressing, following a method he had seen used in the shipyards on the Ouse. It entailed cutting down nearly the whole of a clump of holly trees not far from the clearing. He then spent some weeks stripping these of their outer bark and peeling off the soft underlying pith, which he cut into sections. He boiled the pith in a small caldron he had brought from the *Virginia* until the fibrous mass was reduced to a thick, viscous liquid, which he reheated and smeared over the vessel's hull.

The *Escape* was eventually completed, but the long tale of its building was inscribed forever on Robinson's flesh. Cuts, burns, scars, bruises, and calluses bore witness to the dogged battle he had waged for so long to produce this uncouth but sturdy-looking boat. There was no builder's time sheet, but his own body was record enough.

He started to collect provisions for the journey, but then put the task aside when he reflected that first he must launch his ship to determine her seaworthiness. The truth was that an obscure misgiving had restrained him from doing this at once, the fear of some unforeseen setback that might destroy all hope of success in this enterprise on which his life depended. He considered the vessel's possible defects. She might, for instance, sink so low in the water as to be unmaneuverable and at the mercy of every ripple, or on the other hand she might turn over at the first puff of wind. His worst nightmare was the picture of her sinking like a stone as soon as she was put on the water, while he stood peering down at her, watching the eddying shape sink ever deeper into the shadow of those green, translucent depths.

After a long hesitation engendered by these terrifying pre-sentiments, he finally made up his mind to proceed with the launching. It did not much surprise him to find that he was quite incapable of dragging the hull, which must weigh over half a ton, down the gently sloping grass and over the sand to the sea. But this first reverse, by compelling him to acknowledge the gravity of a problem which hitherto he had scarcely considered, threw a sudden light on the trans-formation which solitude was effecting in his own personal-ity. His field of concentration seemed to be both deepening and narrowing. He was finding it increasingly difficult to think of more than one thing at a time, or even to transfer his attention from one thing to another. He discovered that for all of us the presence of other people is a powerful ele-ment of distraction, not only because they constantly break into our activities and interrupt our train of thought, but because the mere possibility of their doing so illumines a world of concerns situated at the edge of our consciousness but capable at any moment of becoming its center. That marginal and almost ghostly presence of things with which he was not immediately concerned had gradually vanished from Robinson's mind. He was now surrounded by objects subject only to the arbitrary law of all or nothing, and thus it was that, being wholly absorbed in the business of building the ship, he had completely overlooked the problem of launching her. In addition, he had been obsessed with the story of the Ark, which had become for him a sort of prototype of the *Escape*. Built on her mountaintop, far from any shore, the Ark had waited for the rising waters to reach her.

The growing panic which at first he had managed to con-trol overwhelmed him when he found that he was unable to slide rollers under the keel in the way he had seen stone pediments moved during the restoration of York Cathedral. The hull was immovable, and in his efforts to lever it he succeeded only in loosening one of the side members. After three days of desperate, fruitless effort, fatigue and frustrated fury nearly drove him out of his senses. Then another possibility occurred to him, a last hope. Since he could not drag the *Escape* to the sea, he must bring the sea to her. All that was required was a canal or "cut" driven from the shore through the rising ground to the place where the hull stood propped on its legs. When it flooded at high water, he would tip the vessel into it. He started digging furiously; but then, his first ardor abating, he paused to consider the practical aspects of the business—the distance of the hull from the shore and above all its height above sea level. His cut would need to be a hundred and twenty yards long and some ten feet wide, and by the time it reached its destination its walls would be more than a hundred feet high. The task was one that he could scarcely hope to complete singlehanded in all that remained of his natural life.

He gave up.

The surface of thick slime, over which clouds of mosquitoes hovered, was stirred by sluggish ripples as a small suckling pig, nothing of it visible but its speckled snout, moved to attach itself to its mother's flank. Several families of peccary had established their wallow in the marshes on the eastern side of the island, and they lay there half-buried in mud during the hottest period of the day. But whereas the indolent sows, motionless as fallen logs, might have been a part of the landscape, their livelier young ceaselessly fidgeted and quarreled, uttering shrill squeaks. At sunset the sow, with considerable effort, would heave her dripping bulk onto a tongue of solid earth while the children struggled with frantic squeals to avoid being sucked into the quicksand she left behind. The party would then move off in single file, causing a great commotion in the dried undergrowth.

Then a human form, like a statue of clay, rose in its turn and made its way through the reeds. Robinson could not have said how long it was since he had left his last shred of clothing on some thornbush. In any case, the thought of sunburn no longer troubled him, since his back, flanks, and thighs were now protected by a thick coating of dried mud. His hair and beard had grown so long that his face was almost invisible beneath their tangled mass. His hands had become mere forepaws used for walking, since it made him giddy to stand upright. His state of physical weakness and the softness of sand and mud, but above all the breaking of some little spring within his soul, had led him to move only on his hands and knees. He knew now that man resembles a person injured in a street riot, who can only stay upright while the crowd packed densely around him continues to prop him up. Exiled from the mass of his fellows, who had sustained him as a part of humanity without his realizing it, he felt that he no longer had the strength to stand on his own feet. He lived on unmentionable foods, gnawing them with his face to the ground. He relieved himself where he lay, and rarely failed to roll in the damp warmth of his own excrement. He moved less and less, and his brief excursions always ended in his return to the mire. Here, in its warm coverlet of slime, his body lost all weight, while the toxic emanations of the stagnant water drugged his mind. Only his eyes, nose, and mouth were active, alert for edible weed and toad spawn drifting on the surface. Rid of all terrestrial bonds, his thoughts in a half stupor pursued vestiges of memory which emerged like phantoms from the past to dance in the blue gaps between the motionless foliage. He remembered silent hours of childhood spent among the bales of wool and cotton in his father's gloomy storeroom. The piled rolls were like a padded fortress absorbing light and sound, drafts of air, and sudden movement. The close, musty air was heavy with the odors of wool grease, dust, and varnish, and also of the aromatic gum which his father used throughout the year to combat a cold that he could never shake off. Robinson had thought he owed nothing except his russet hair to that nervous, self-effacing little man whose life was spent at a high desk poring over his account books, and that all his other qualities came from his mother, who was a wonderful woman. The mire, by demonstrating his capacity for turning inward upon himself and withdrawing from the external world, had shown him that he had inherited more than he thought from that little draper in York.

In his long hours of cloudy meditation he evolved a philosophy which might have been his father's own. Only the past had any worth or existence deserving of note. The present was valueless except as the repository of memories accumulated in the past, and to add to that increasing fund was the only reason for living. In the end came death; and death itself was no more than the long-awaited moment when this treasure might be wholly enjoyed. Eternity was bestowed on us so that we might relive our life in death, more observantly, more intelligently, and more sensually than was possible in the turmoil of the present.

He was browsing on watercress in the bed of a small stream when he heard the sound of music, unreal yet distinct, like a celestial symphony, a chorus of crystalline voices accompanied by the strings of a harp and a viola da gamba. He thought at first that it was indeed heavenly music, meaning that his life was approaching its end, if indeed he were not already dead. But then, looking out to sea, he saw the white gleam of a sail on the eastern horizon. Springing to his feet he ran to the building yard of the *Escape*, where he had left his tools lying, and by good fortune found his flint and steel almost at once. He ran to the eucalyptus tree, and, setting fire to a bundle of dry twigs, thrust it into an aperture at the bottom of the hollow trunk. A cloud of acrid smoke rose up, but the huge conflagration which he had counted on was slow to materialize.

In any case, what did it matter? The ship was heading for the island on a course that would bring it into the Bay of Salvation. It must surely intend to anchor and send a boat ashore. Uttering demented cries, Robinson dashed madly about in search of a shirt and pair of trousers, which eventually he found stowed away under the *Escape*'s hull. Then he ran down to the shore, clawing at his face as though to remove the dense mat of hair that covered it. Swaying gracefully in the northeasterly breeze, the ship was drawing near the breakers running up the beach. She was one of those old-time Spanish galleons whose function had been to bring home to Spain the treasures of the New World, and it seemed to Robinson that below the water line, as she heeled, her lower strakes were indeed the color of gold. She was under full sail, and from the head of her mainmast a double-pointed pennant of black and yellow fluttered in the breeze. As she drew near Robinson saw a brilliant company assembled on her forecastle and main deck.

It seemed that some high festivity was in progress. The

music came from a small string orchestra and a choir of children in white robes grouped on the quarter-deck. Men and women were elegantly dancing around a table loaded with dishes of gold and crystal goblets. No one seemed to see the shipwrecked man or even the shore, with which the ship was now sailing parallel, having altered course only a cable length away. Robinson kept abreast of her, running over the sand, shouting, waving his arms, pausing to pick up sticks of wood which he flung in her direction. He stumbled, picked himself up, and fell again. She was now coming level with the first of the sand dunes and he was held up by the lagoons at that end of the beach. He plunged into the water and swam with all his strength, seeing no more of the ship than her receding stern and aftercastle draped with brocade. A young girl was leaning out of a cabin window, and with a dazzling clarity Robinson saw her face. It was a very young face, tender and vulnerable, yet seeming already touched by experience, and illumined with a pale, skeptical, forlorn smile. Robinson knew that face. He was sure of it. But who was the child? He opened his mouth to cry out to her, and salt water poured down his throat. A green dusk enveloped him just as he caught sight of the grimacing mask of a small skate which, swimming backward, fled away from him.

A fiery column roused him from his torpor. He was horribly cold. Had the sea flung him a second time on the same stretch of beach? High above him, on the western cliff, the eucalyptus was blazing like a torch in the darkness, and he staggered upward toward that source of warmth and light.

By a supreme irony the signal beacon that was to have

shone out over the ocean, summoning the rest of mankind, had attracted no one to it but himself!

He spent the night huddled in the bushes, his eyes fixed on the pit of incandescence, shot with vivid color, that opened up at the base of the tree; and as the heat died down he drew closer. Not until the early hours of the morning was he able to give a name, a Christian name at that, to the girl on the galleon. She was his younger sister, Lucy, who had died some ten years ago. Now he could no longer doubt that that vessel of a bygone age had been the vision of a disordered mind.

He got to his feet and stood looking out over the sea. That metallic surface, glittering already under the first rays of the sun, had been his temptation, his snare, and his drug. Only a little more was needed to degrade him utterly and drive him to the depths of madness. Under pain of death he must find the strength to tear himself away from it. The island lay behind him, huge and untrodden, filled with limited promises and harsh lessons. He must once again take his life in hand. He must work. With no more dreaming he must consummate his marriage with solitude, his implacable bride.

Turning his back on the ocean, he picked his way up the slope of rubble, overgrown with silvery thistles, that led to the center of the island.

CHAPTER THREE

Robinson spent the next few weeks making a methodical survey of the island and taking stock of its resources—its edible plants, potentially useful animals, fresh-water springs, and natural shelters. By good fortune the shell of the *Virginia* had not been entirely demolished by the spells of bad weather during the preceding weeks, although parts of the deck and timbering had been carried away. So had the bodies of the captain and the lookout man, and this was a relief to Robinson, although it caused him pangs of conscience. He had promised them a grave: instead, he would build them a cenotaph. He made the cave in the rocky tor at the center of the island his general storeroom, and here he transferred everything he could remove from the wreck, rejecting nothing movable, because even the most useless objects now possessed for him the value of relics, links with the human community from which he was sundered. After installing the barrels of black powder in the depths of the cave, he brought in three chests of clothes, five sacks of grain, two baskets of crockery and tableware, several cases of miscellaneous objects—candlesticks, spurs, ornaments, spectacles, pocketknives, charts, mirrors, dice, and so on— various jugs and drinking vessels, and a box of gear which included wire cable, blocks, lamps, marlinespikes, fishing line, floats, and other possibly useful equipment; and finally he brought ashore a small strongbox containing gold, silver, and copper coins. The few books he found on board were so damaged by sea water that the print was unreadable, but it occurred to him that if he dried them in the sun their whitened pages might serve him for a diary, if he could find something to use as ink. This deficiency was unexpectedly supplied by a fish which was to be found in shoals at the foot of the cliffs on the eastern side of the island. The sea porcupine, which is dreaded for its strong, densely toothed jaws and the poisonous prickles that rise along its spine when it is alarmed, possesses the curious faculty of being able to blow itself up like a ball. The air is collected in its stomach, and in this condition it swims on its back without seeming in any way inconvenienced by its eccentric posture. Robinson found, when he turned one over as it was lying on the beach, that anything coming in contact with the skin of its stomach, whether distended or slack, was stained brilliant red with a remarkably lasting dye. The flesh was highly palatable, as firm and delicately flavored as chicken. After catching a large number of these fish, Robinson squeezed the excretion from their skins into a cloth and thus provided himself with a somewhat evil-smelling but entirely serviceable red ink. He then cut himself a quill from a vulture's feather, and nearly wept with delight when he traced his first words on paper. In performing the sacred act of writing it seemed to him that he had half-retrieved himself from the abyss of animalism into which he had sunk, and returned to the world of the spirit. From then on he opened his journal nearly every day, not to set down the greater or lesser events of the day, to which he attached little importance, but to record his thoughts, his spiritual progress, his recollections of the past and the reflections to which these gave rise.

A new life began for him—or, more exactly, it was the beginning of his true life on the island, after that period of degradation which he now thought of with shame and sought to forget. This explains why, having at length resolved to keep a calendar, he was little troubled by the fact that he had no means of determining how long he had been on the island. The wreck of the *Virginia* had occurred during the night of September 30, 1759, at about two o'clock in the morning. Between that date and the day when he first cut a notch in the trunk of a pine tree, there stretched an indefinite and incalculable period of shadow and despair. Robinson felt himself cut off from the human calendar as much as he was separated from mankind by the expanse of waters, reduced to living on an island in time as well as in space.

He spent several days drawing a map, which he subsequently amplified and amended as his knowledge of the island increased. He decided to rechristen it, having from the day of his arrival bestowed on it the opprobrium of that heavy name, the Island of Desolation. Being struck during his reading of the Bible by the admirable paradox whereby the Christian religion makes despair the unforgivable sin and hope one of the three cardinal virtues, he resolved to call it Speranza, the Island of Hope, a tuneful, sunny word which, moreover, evoked the wholly profane memory of a hot-blooded Italian girl whom he had known when he was a student at York University. The simplicity and depth of his religious faith readily accepted these correlations, which a more superficial mind might have held to be blasphemous. It also struck him, poring over his rough map, that viewed from a certain angle the island resembled a female body, headless but nevertheless a woman, seated with her legs drawn up beneath her in an attitude wherein submission, fear, and simple abandonment were inextricably mingled. The thought passed through his mind and was forgotten; but later he would return to it.

An examination of the sacks of grain he had brought from the *Virginia*, containing rice, wheat, barley, and maize, caused him severe disappointment. Rats and weevils had eaten a considerable part, leaving nothing but the husks and their droppings, and a good deal of the rest was moldy. After laboriously separating the good from the bad, grain by grain, he found that, apart from the rice, which was undamaged but uncultivable, he had retrieved ten gallons of wheat, six of barley, and four of maize. He resolved to sow it, for he attached infinite value to bread, the symbol of life, the only food mentioned in the Lord's Prayer, as he did to everything that still linked him with the community of mankind. And he felt that bread yielded by the soil of Speranza would be tangible proof that she accepted him, as he had accepted this nameless island on whose shores chance had cast him.

He set fire to several acres of grassland on a day when the wind was blowing from the west, and, after breaking up the surface with a hoe—improvised from the sheet of metal brought from the *Virginia*, in which he had contrived to pierce a hole large enough to take a handle—he sowed crops of wheat, maize, and barley. He vowed to treat his first harvest as a benefaction bestowed by Nature—that is to say, by God—on the labor of his hands.

Of the animals inhabiting the island, the goats, which were numerous, would certainly be the most valuable if he could domesticate them. The kids were quite approachable, but the mothers resisted fiercely when he tried to milk them. Ac-

cordingly he built a fenced enclosure of saplings, tied and
interwoven with lianas. He drove a few young kids into
this, and the mothers followed. He then turned the kids out,
and before long the fullness of their udders caused the mothers to welcome milking. In short, after cultivating the soil
of the island, he had now given it the beginnings of a dairy
herd. Like mankind at the dawn of history, he had passed
through the stage of hunting and gathering into that of tilling
and stock raising.

But he was still far from thinking of the island as a wilderness which he might conquer and subdue until he had made it
a wholly human place of habitation. Not a day went by
without some unexpected or hurtful incident occurring to
remind him of the anguish he had felt when, realizing that
he was the only survivor of the wreck, he had seen himself
the orphan of mankind. The sense of his forlorn state, although it was allayed by the sight of his tilled fields, his
goat pen, his well-ordered storeroom and imposing array of
weapons, brought a lump to his throat on the day when he
saw a vampire bat crouched over the throat of a kid whose
blood it was sucking. The creature's taloned and tattered
wings enfolded the small animal like a cloak of death as it
swayed weakly on its legs. On another occasion, when he
was gathering shellfish on some half-submerged rocks, he
was hit by a jet of water in the face. Slightly dazed by the
shock, he moved forward, only to be checked by a second
jet, aimed with uncanny precision. At once he was assailed
by that familiar and dreaded sense of alienation, which was
only partly relieved when he discovered, in a cavity in the
rocks, a small, gray squid which possessed the remarkable
gift of being able to squirt water like a siphon in any direction it chose.

He eventually became resigned to the remorseless scrutiny of his "governing board," as he termed the group of vultures who seemed to have attached themselves permanently to him. No matter where he went or what he did they kept him company, hunchbacked, goitrous, and bald, watching and waiting—not, indeed, for his death, as he had at first believed in his moments of depression, but for the edible fragments he scattered in the course of the day. But although he had of necessity grown used to their presence, he found it less easy to endure their repulsive habits. Their love commerce, like that of lubricious old men, offended his enforced chastity. Filled with outraged melancholy he watched the male, after a few grotesque skips, heavily tread the female, sinking its hooked beak into her bare, blood-red neck while their rumps came together in an obscene embrace. One day he noticed that a smaller and doubtless younger bird was being harried and ill-treated by several of the others. They pecked it and beat it with their wings, finally surrounding it and driving it against a rock. Then abruptly the hostilities ceased, as though the victim had cried mercy or in some way let it be known that it submitted to the demands of its persecutors. With its neck stretched stiffly toward the ground, the small vulture advanced a few paces, stopped, and, shaken by internal spasms, regurgitated a decomposing and half-digested gob of meat, evidently the proceeds of a private act of gluttony which its companions had detected. They fell upon the nauseous mess and devoured it, jostling each other.

This occurred on a morning when Robinson had broken his hoe and allowed his best milch goat to get away. It completed his demoralization. For the first time in months he had a relapse and yielded to the temptation of the mire. Following the track of the wild pigs leading to the marshland on the east side of the island, he returned to the swamp where he had come so near to losing his reason, and, stripping off his clothes, he let his body sink into the tepid slime.

By degrees the nightmare of squids, vampire bats, and vultures which obsessed his mind vanished into that mephitic mist filled with the drone of mosquitoes. Time and space dissolved, and a face appeared in the clouded sky, bordered with foliage, which was the only thing he could see. He dreamed that he was lying in a gently rocking cradle roofed with a curtain of muslin, and his tiny hands were all that emerged from the lily-white swaddling clothes that enclosed him. Around him a murmur of words and domestic sounds recalled the familiar setting of the house where he was born. The firm, controlled voice of his mother mingled with the shriller, always querulous tones of his father, and the laughter of his brothers and sisters. He did not understand what they were saying, or seek to understand. The embroidered veil parted to reveal the slender face of Lucy, rendered narrower still by the two heavy plaits of dark hair, one of which fell upon his coverlet. Weakness pervaded Robinson, exquisitely sweet. A smile parted his lips, amid the rotting grass and water-lily leaves. A small leech had attached itself to the corner of his mouth.

Journal

Each man has his slippery slope. Mine leads to the mire. That is where Speranza drives me when she grows evil and shows me her animal face. The mire is my defeat, my vice. My victory is the moral order I must impose on Speranza against her natural order, which is but another name for total disorder. I know now that in this place it cannot be solely a question of survival. Merely to survive is to die. It is a matter of building, organizing, ordering, patiently and without cease. Every pause is a backward step, a step toward the mire.

The strange circumstances in which I find myself must, I think, warrant many changes in my thinking, notably in moral and religious matters. I read the Bible daily, and every day I lend an attentive ear to the voice of wisdom that speaks in me as it does in every man. I am sometimes startled by the novelty of my discoveries, but I accept them nevertheless, for no custom must be allowed to prevail over the voice of the Holy Spirit which resides in all of us.

Thus it is with Vice and Virtue. My upbringing taught me to see in Vice an excess and extravagance, a debauch and overflowing, to which Virtue opposed humility, self-effacement, and self-denial. I find that this kind of morality is a luxury which would cause my death if I sought to follow it. My present situation requires that I should set wider bounds to Virtue and diminish those of Vice, regarding as virtues courage, strength, self-assertion, and mastery over the external world. Vice is renunciation, self-abandonment, submission—in a word, the mire. No doubt this is to retreat beyond Christianity to a more ancient vision of human wisdom, and to substitute virtus for virtue. But at the root of a certain kind of Christianity there lies the radical rejection of Nature and earthly things, a rejection which I have practiced to excess in regard to Speranza, and which has nearly been my downfall. I shall triumph over defeat to the extent that I am able to accept my island and cause it to accept me.

As his mortification at the failure of the *Escape* died down, Robinson came to think more and more of the advantages of possessing a small, light craft in which he might explore those parts of the island's coast which could not be reached by land. Accordingly he set about hollowing a shell canoe out of a pine trunk—slow, monotonous work with the ax, at which he toiled methodically for a set period every day, but with none of the feverish excitement he had brought to the building of the *Escape*. He had thought at first of building a fire under a part of the trunk, but he was afraid that the whole of it would become charred, and he merely lit a fire out of kindling in the hollow he had begun. In the end he abandoned the use of fire altogether. Adequately hollowed, shaped and smoothed with fine sand, the canoe was sufficiently light for him to be able to lift it on his back and carry it down to the sea like a great wooden helmet. The first sight of it dancing on the waves was as enchanting to him as the sight of a young foal skipping in a meadow. He had made himself a double-ended paddle, being inhibited from attempting any kind of sail by the recollection of his overambitious efforts with the *Escape*. He made a series of excursions around the island which completed his knowledge of his domain, but which made him realize, more than anything else he had done, the extent of his absolute solitude.

Journal

Solitude is not a changeless state imposed on me by the wreck of the Virginia. *It is a corrosive influence which acts on me slowly but ceaselessly, and in one sense purely destruc-*

tively. On my first day here I was divided between two human societies, both imaginary—the vanished crew and the people of the island, which I supposed to be inhabited. I was still warm from contact with my fellow men, continuing in my mind the dialogue cut short by the disaster. Then the island turned out to be deserted. I was in a land bereft of humankind. The group of my unfortunate companions receded into darkness, and their voices had long been silent when my own was still only beginning to weary of its soliloquy. Since then I have noted with a horrid fascination the dehumanizing process which I feel to be inexorably at work within me.

I know now that every man carries within himself—and as it were above himself—a fragile and complex framework of habits, responses, reflexes, preoccupations, dreams, and associations, formed and constantly transformed by perpetual contact with his fellows. Deprived of its sap, this delicate growth withers and dissolves. My fellow men were the mainstay of my world. . . . Each day I measure my debt to them by observing the fresh cracks in my personal structure. I know what I would suffer should I lose the use of words, and with all the power of my anguish I seek to combat that final surrender. But my relationship to material things is also undermined by solitude. When a painter or engraver introduces human figures into a landscape or alongside a monument, they are not there merely as an accessory. Human figures convey the scale, and what is still more important, they represent attitudes, possible points of view, which enrich the picture for the outside observer by providing him with other, indispensable points of reference.

But in Speranza there is only one viewpoint, my own, deprived of all context. And this shedding of context was not completed in a day. At first, and as it were instinctively, I projected possible observers—parameters—onto hilltops or behind rocks or into the branches of trees. The island was thus charted by a network of interpolations and extrapolations which lent it different aspects and rendered it meaningful. That is what every normal man does in a normal situation. I became aware of this function—with many others—only when I found it dying within me. Today the process is complete. My vision of the island is reduced to that of my own eyes, and what I do not see of it is to me a total unknown. Everywhere I am not total darkness reigns. I find, indeed, as I write these lines, that the experience I am seeking to define is not only without precedent, but that it contradicts in their essence the very words I am using. Language in a fundamental manner evokes the peopled world, where other men are like so many lamps casting a glow of light around them within which everything is, if not known, at least knowable. Those lights have vanished from my consciousness. For a long time, fed by my fantasy, they continued to reach me. Now it is over, and the darkness has closed in.

But my solitude does not only destroy the meaning of things. It undermines them at the very root of their being. More and more I find myself doubting the evidence of my senses. I know now that the very earth beneath my feet needs to be trodden by feet other than mine if I am to be sure of its substance. Optical illusions, mirages, hallucinations, waking dreams, imagined sounds, fantasy and delirium . . . against these aberrations the surest guard is our brother, our neighbor, our friend, or our enemy—anyway, God save us, someone. . . .

Yesterday, on my way through the small wood leading

*to the grasslands on the southeastern coast, I was brought to
a standstill by a smell which took me suddenly and almost
painfully back to my father's house, to the office where he
was in the habit of receiving customers; but this was a
Monday morning, the day when visitors were not admitted
and when my mother, helped by one of the neighbors, polished the floor. The impression was so powerful, so incon-
gruous, that once again I doubted my reason. For a moment
I struggled against that memory, which was one of over-
powering sweetness; then I let my thoughts slip back into
the past, to that empty museum, that dead world, varnished
like a coffin, which called to me with such seductive tenderness. Finally the illusion loosed its hold on me. Walking on
through the wood, I came upon some shrubs of terebinth,
of which the bark, cracking in the heat, exuded an amber-
colored resin whose powerful odor had evoked all the Monday mornings of my childhood.*

Because it was a Tuesday morning, Robinson, in accordance with his work schedule, was on a strip of beach newly
uncovered by the tide, collecting a particular kind of clam
with rather tough flesh but a pleasant flavor, which he could
keep for a week by storing in a jar of sea water. He wore
a round British seaman's hat, a pair of wooden clogs, breeches
which left his calves bare, and a loose cotton shirt. The sun,
which bit into his pale, redhead's skin, was veiled by a curtain of cloud lumpy as astrakhan, and he had been able to
leave his parasol in the cave, although he seldom went anywhere without it. It was low water, and after crossing over
beds of broken shells, strips of mud, and shallow pools, he

had come a sufficient distance from Speranza to be able to see
the island's green, yellow, and black mass as a whole. Having
no one else to talk to, he discoursed with her in a slow,
deep dialogue in which his movements, his acts and undertakings were so many questions to which she replied with
the favor or disfavor that befell them. He no longer doubted
that everything must henceforth depend on his relations with
Speranza and his success in ordering their joint affairs. He
was always on the alert for her responses, which came to
him in a thousand forms, sometimes ciphered, sometimes
symbolic.

He came to a flat, weed-covered rock surrounded by a
pool of clear water, and he was amusedly watching the
antics of a small, intrepid crab which was defying him with
two upraised pincers of unequal size, like a hired assassin
with sword and dagger, when he was struck dumb with
amazement at seeing the imprint of a naked foot. It would
not have surprised him to come upon his own traces in the
sand or mud, although he had long since given up going
without clogs, but this footprint was sunk into *the rock
itself*. Was it that of some other man? Or had he been on
the island so long that the imprint of his foot in the sandy
slime covering the rock had had time to become petrified?
He took off his right clog and set his foot in the imprint,
which was half-filled with sea water. That was precisely
what it was. His foot fitted the imprint as though he were
putting on a well-worn slipper. There could be no doubt
about it, no fantasy or mystification; it was not Adam's footprint when he had taken possession of the Garden, or that of
Venus rising from the sea; it was his personal signature and
his alone, impressed in the living rock, indelible and eternal.

Like one of the free-ranging cattle herds on the Argentine pampas, which bear the mark of the branding iron, Speranza bore the seal of her lord and master.

The maize crop had failed completely, and the plot of land where Robinson had sown it was reverting to its original, overgrown state. But the wheat and barley were both doing well, and Robinson experienced the first delight Speranza had given him—how sweet it was!—when he caressed those tender, blue-tinted shoots. It took great strength of mind to refrain from pulling out the weeds that here and there disfigured his neatly ordered rows, but he could not infringe the biblical injunction which lays down that the good grain must not be separated from the tares before the harvest. He consoled himself with the thought of the golden loaves he would soon be bringing out of the oven he had carved in the soft stone in a wall of the cave. A brief spell of rainy weather caused him to tremble for the slender stalks as they bowed under the burden of heavy heads weighted with water. But then the sun shone again and they stood upright, swaying in the breeze like an army of small horses curvetting with plumed headgear.

When the time came for harvesting Robinson decided, since he had no scythe or sickle, that the most appropriate of the few implements he possessed was the old boarding cutlass he had retrieved from the *Virginia*, where it had hung in the captain's cabin. His first thought had been to proceed in an orthodox fashion, using a stick to hold the stalks upright while the blade swept through them. But as he took that warlike weapon in his hand a strange frenzy seized him, and, forgetting the rules, he slashed about him in all directions, furiously shouting as he did so. Not many of the heads were damaged by this treatment, but he lost a good deal of the straw.

Journal

That harvest day, which should have celebrated the first fruits of my labor and the fruitfulness of Speranza, was more like a desperate battle against nothing. How far I still am from the perfect life in which every action is governed by the laws of economy and harmony! I let myself be carried away like a child in an outburst of disorder, and I recaptured none of the lighthearted joys I had known when haymaking in the West Riding. The rhythmic movement, the swing of the arms from right to left which the body balances by swaying from left to right, the scythe blade cutting into the yielding, flowery mass and laying its swath at my left hand, the heady scent of juice and sap—all this constituted a simple happiness in which I could delight without repining. The whetted blades were so supple that they could be seen to bend first one way and then the other. The meadow was a growing mass to be attacked and conquered, methodically laid low, step by step and line by line. But it was an intricately contrived mass, an array of minute living entities, a vegetable world in which matter was wholly subjected to form. That infinite variety of the European meadow is the exact opposite of the amorphous, undifferentiated herbage I cut down here. Nature in the tropics is powerful, but crude and simple as the glaring blue sky. Alas, when shall I again see our pale skies and the exquisite grays of the mist rising over the valley of the Ouse?

Having threshed his wheat and barley by flailing it in a sail folded in two, Robinson winnowed the grain by pouring it from one container into another on a windy day, letting the husks and chaff blow where they would. He enjoyed that work of purification, simple but not wearisome, for the spiritual symbols it evoked. His spirit rose up to God, beseeching Him to cause the frivolous thoughts that filled his mind to scatter in the winds, leaving behind only the solid seeds of wisdom. When the winnowing was done he found with pride that his harvest amounted to thirty gallons of wheat and twenty of barley. He had prepared a mortar and pestle to grind his flour—a hollowed tree stump and a heavy branch knotted at one end—and the fire beneath the oven was laid in readiness for the first baking. And then, on a sudden impulse, he resolved to eat none of that first crop.

Journal

I had been keenly looking forward to the first loaf to come out of the soil of Speranza, out of my oven and the labor of my hands. But it must wait till later. Later . . . The wealth of promise in that simple word! What suddenly dawned upon me with an overwhelming certainty is my need to fight against time, that is to say, to imprison time. Insofar as I live from day to day, I let myself drift; time slips through my fingers, and in losing time I lose myself. Indeed, the whole problem of this island may be expressed in terms of time, and it is no accident if, at the lowest level, I started by living here as though I were outside time. When I began a calendar I regained possession of myself. But now I must do more. None of this first harvest of wheat and barley must be swallowed up by the present. It must be preserved as a source of strength for the future. I shall divide it into two parts, one part seed for the next sowing and the other a provision for contingencies, for the second harvest might be ruined.

Henceforth I shall abide by the following rule: all production is creation, therefore good; all consumption is destruction, therefore bad. My situation is, in fact, not unlike that of my fellow countrymen who land by shiploads on the coasts of the New World. They too must bow to the law of accumulation. For them too the wasting of time is a crime and the saving of time a cardinal virtue. To accumulate! Once again I am reminded of the wretchedness of my solitude. Where I am concerned, to sow and reap is good: the evil sets in when I grind and knead and bake, for then I am working only for myself. The American colonist need have no misgivings about making bread; he will sell the bread, and the money he stores in his chest represents the saving of time and work. But I in my solitude am deprived of the benefits of money, although I have no lack of it.

Today I can measure the folly and malice of those who affect to despise money, that divine institution. Money spiritualizes all that it touches by endowing it with a quality that is both rational (measurable) and universal, since property reckoned in terms of money is accessible to all men. Venality is one of the cardinal virtues. The venal man suppresses his murderous and anti-social instincts—honor, self-pride, patriotism, political ambition, religious fanaticism, racialism—in favor of his need to co-operate with others, his love of fruitful exchanges, his sense of human solidarity. The term, the Golden Age, should be taken literally, and I see now that mankind would swiftly achieve it were its *affairs wholly in the hands of venal men. Alas, it is nearly always high-minded men who make history, and so the flames destroy everything and blood flows in torrents. The plump merchants of Venice afford us an example of the luxurious happiness possible in a state governed solely by the law of lucre, whereas the emaciated wolves of the Spanish Inquisition show us the infamies of which men are capable when they have lost the love of material well-being. The Huns would soon have checked their advance if they had known how to profit by the riches they acquired. Encumbered with their gains, they would have stayed to enjoy them, and life would have resumed its course. But they were disinterested savages. They despised gold. They rushed onward, burning as they went.*

Thereafter Robinson entered on a course of frugal living while he labored intensively to develop the island's resources. He cleared and tilled whole acres of meadow and forest, sowed a field of turnips, sorrel, and other vegetables that grew sporadically in the south, protected newly planted palm trees against the depredations of birds and insects, set up a dozen skeps which were gradually occupied by wild bees, and near the water's edge dug ponds of salt and fresh water in which he bred bream and angelfish and even sea shrimps. He laid in huge stores of dried fruit, smoked meat, salt fish, and small cheeses which were hard and gritty as chalk but kept indefinitely. And finally he discovered a method of producing a kind of sugar with which to make jam and preserve fruit. It was derived from a variety of palm, thicker in the middle than at the top or bottom, which exuded a great quantity of very sweet sap. Felling one of these trees, he cut off its crown of foliage, and the sap immediately began to ooze out of its upper end. It continued to do this for some months, but he had to cut off a fresh slice every day, because the pores had a tendency to close. A single tree gave him ninety gallons of this molasses, which solidified into an enormous cake.

Journal

Tenn, my faithful shipmate, has returned to me. I find it impossible to express the happiness contained in those words. I shall never know where or how he has been living since the wreck, but at least I think I can understand what caused him to avoid me. He appeared while I was working like a madman on the Escape, only to beat an instant retreat, furiously growling. In my blindness I wondered whether the terror of the shipwreck, followed by a long period of solitude in hostile country, had not caused him to revert to the savage state. Incredible complacency! It was I who was the savage, not he, and I cannot doubt that my wild expression and frenzied manner terrified the poor creature, who had remained more civilized than I. There is no lack of instances of dogs who have been compelled almost against their will to desert a master sunk in the depths of degradation or folly, and I know of none which would allow its master to eat out of the same bowl as itself. Tenn's return rejoices my heart because it testifies to my victory over the destructive forces which were dragging me toward the abyss. The dog is the natural companion of man, but not of the noisome and degenerate creature which misfortune, stripping him of human semblance, may make of him. Henceforth I shall read in Tenn's trusting eyes whether I am capable of preserving my human stature despite the fate that threatens to destroy me.

But Robinson could not wholly regain his human dignity except by providing himself with a better dwelling than a cave or a screen of leaves. Now that he had as companion the most *domesticated* of all animals, he needed to build himself a proper setting for domesticity, a *domus*, a house.

He decided to build it near the entrance to the cave where all his wealth was stored, which was also at the highest point of the island. He began by digging a wide, rectangular trench some three feet deep, which he filled with branches covered with a deep layer of white sand. On this well-drained foundation he set up walls of palm logs, notched and fitted together, the interstices being filled by their scaly bark with its growth of vegetable matting. He constructed a double-sided roof of light poles plaited with reed which he covered with the leaves of rubber plants, using them like slates. Then he plastered the outside of the walls with a mortar made of clay and chopped straw, and completed his sand floor with a rough paving of flat stones, over which he spread goatskins and straw mats. A few articles of furniture made of osier, the dishes and lanterns he had retrieved from the *Virginia*, the spyglass, the cutlass, and one of the muskets hanging on the wall created an atmosphere of comfort and even intimacy in which he constantly rejoiced. Seen from outside, that first dwelling had the surprising look of a tropical log cabin, crude but neat, with a fragile roof but massive walls, which seemed to Robinson a mirror of the paradox in his own situation. He was conscious both of its practical in-

adequacy and of its symbolic, and above all moral, importance. He soon resolved not to use it for any workaday
purpose, not even for cooking, and only to sleep in it on
Saturday nights, continuing during the rest of the week to
sleep on the litter of straw and feathers which he had installed in the alcove he had dug in the rocky wall of the
cave. By degrees the cabin became for him a sort of museum
of civilized living, and he never entered it without a certain
sense of ritual. He even fell into the habit—having unpacked
the garments contained in the chests brought from the *Virginia*, some of which were very handsome—of entering it
only in suitable attire, wearing jacket, breeches, stockings,
and shoes, as though he were paying a formal call on all
that was best in himself.

He later realized that the sun was visible from inside the
building only at certain hours of the day, and that he needed
something to measure the passing of time. Accordingly, after
a number of experiments, he contrived a primitive clepsydra,
or water clock, out of a glass demijohn in the bottom of
which he pierced a very small hole through which the water
escaped, drop by drop, into a brass bowl beneath it. By
trial and error he found the precise amount of water needed
for it to empty itself in twenty-four hours, and he then
marked the hours in rings round the jar, numbering them
with Roman numerals. This water clock was an immense
comfort to him. Listening by day and night to the regular
"plop" of water dropping into the bowl, he had the feeling
that time could no longer slip away from him, that he had
regulated and mastered time—in a word, tamed it, just as
the whole island was gradually to be tamed by the strength
and resolution of a single man.

Journal

Henceforth, whether I am waking or sleeping, writing or cooking a meal, my time is marked by this regular ticking, positive, unanswerable, measurable, and precise. How eagerly I seek those adjectives which for me represent so many victories over the forces of evil! I demand, I insist, that everything around me shall henceforth be measured, tested, certified, mathematical, and rational. One of my tasks must be to make a full survey of the island, its distances and its contours, and incorporate all these details in an accurate surveyor's map. I would like every plant to be labeled, every bird to be ringed, every animal to be branded. I shall not be content until this opaque and impenetrable place, filled with secret ferments and malignant stirrings, has been transformed into a rational structure, visible and intelligible to its very depths!

But shall I have the strength to complete this formidable task? Do I possess in myself the massive dose of rationality I wish to administer to Speranza? The regular plop of the clepsydra, which a moment ago soothed me with its deliberate, consoling music, like the ticking of a metronome, now brings to mind a different, terrifying image: the inexorable dripping of water that can wear away a stone. I cannot dismiss it from my mind, and my whole philosophy trembles. The disintegration of language is the most obvious sign of this erosion.

Although I constantly talk aloud, never letting an observation or an idea enter my head without proclaiming it to the trees or the clouds, I note with every day that passes the collapse of whole sectors of that citadel of words within which our thought dwells and moves, like a mole in its network of tunnels. Those fixed points which thought uses for its progression, like crossing a river on steppingstones, are crumbling and vanishing beneath the surface. I am losing my sense of the meaning of words which do not refer to concrete objects. I can only talk literally. Metaphor, litotes, and hyperbole call for an exaggerated effort of concentration that only emphasizes everything absurd and arbitrary in these figures of speech. I can imagine that this mental travail would be of extreme interest to a grammarian or philologist; but to me it is a useless and destructive luxury. For example, the notion of depth, which I never troubled to scrutinize when using it in such expressions as "a deep thinker" or "a deep love." It is a strange prejudice which sets a higher value on depth than on breadth, and which accepts "superficial" as meaning not "of wide extent" but "of little depth," whereas "deep," on the other hand, signifies "of great depth" and not "of small surface." Yet it seems to me that a feeling such as love is better measured, if it can be measured at all, by the extent of its surface than by its degree of depth. For I measure my love for a woman by the fact that I love indiscriminately her hands, her eyes, her carriage, the clothes she wears, the commonplace things she merely touches, the place where she dwells, the sea in which she bathes. . . . All this, it seems to me, is decidedly on the surface! Whereas a lesser love aims directly—in depth—at sex, and leaves all the rest in a shadowy background.

A similar process of thought—which has recently begun to grate on me when I seek to apply it—prefers the inward to the outward being. Men are regarded as riches enclosed in a worthless shell, and the more deeply we penetrate within *them, the greater is the treasure we discover. But what if there were no treasure? What if the statue were solid, filled with a dull sameness like a doll stuffed with husks? I know only too well—I to whom no one comes to lend me a countenance or enrich me with secrets—that I am no more than an emptiness in the heart of Speranza, an attitude to Speranza—a viewpoint, a nothing. I think the soul only acquires any notable content from beyond that barrier of skin which separates the inner from the outer world, and that it enriches itself only inasmuch as it flows out in widening circles from that central point which is Me. Robinson can be infinitely rich only when he merges with Speranza as a whole.*

On the following day Robinson laid the foundations of a Conservatory of Weights and Measures. He built it in the form of a pavilion, but out of the most durable materials he could find, blocks of granite with bondstones of laterite. In it he displayed, on a sort of altar, as though they were idols, and on the walls—like a panoply of the weapons of reason—the measures of an inch, a foot, a yard, a rod, a cable length, a pint, a peck, a bushel, a gallon, a grain, a dram, an ounce, and a pound avoirdupois.

CHAPTER FOUR

On the day 1000 of his calendar, Robinson dressed himself in formal attire and closed the door of his official Residence. Standing at a desk which he had designed so he could write in an upright position, and in an attitude of solemn formality, he wrote in the largest of the sea-washed volumes he had brought off the *Virginia:*

CHARTER OF THE ISLAND OF SPERANZA INAUGURATED ON THE 1000TH DAY OF THE LOCAL CALENDAR.

ARTICLE THE FIRST. *By virtue of the Inspiration of the Holy Spirit, interpreted and obeyed in conformity with the teachings of the Revered Friend, George Fox, subject of His Majesty King George II, Robinson Crusoe, born at York on the 19th December, 1737, is hereby appointed Governor of the Island of Speranza, situated in the Pacific Ocean between the Islands of Juan Fernández and the coast of Chile. As holder of this Office he has full Powers of Legislation and Execution throughout the Territory of the Island and its territorial waters, in accordance with the dictates of the Inner Light.*

ARTICLE II. *The inhabitants of the island are required to express aloud all such thoughts as may occur to them, in a clear and audible voice.*

Gloss. *The loss of the faculty of speech through lack of prac-* \
tice is among the most humiliating disasters that threaten me.
Already when I speak aloud I am conscious of a thickness
of the tongue, as though after an excess of wine. It is important
therefore that the inward discourse which we pursue in our
minds during all our conscious moments should be spoken by
my lips, that they may be constantly exercised. This is indeed
a natural tendency, and it calls for perpetual vigilance lest the
words be uttered before the thought is formulated, as hap-
pens with children and old people who babble aloud in the
weakness of their wits. /

ARTICLE III. *It is forbidden to perform one's natural functions*
except in the places reserved for that purpose.
Gloss. *That this ordinance should rank as Article III of the*
Charter may cause surprise. But the Governor must legislate
in the light of necessity as it presents itself, and in view of the
moral laxity that menaces the inhabitants of the island it is
essential that some small discipline should be imposed on them
in that area of their life which most closely approaches
bestiality.

ARTICLE IV. *Friday is a day of fasting.*

ARTICLE V. *Sunday is a day of rest. At seven o'clock on Saturday*
evening all work on the island will cease and the inhabitants will
don their best attire for dinner. On Sunday morning at ten they
will gather in the Meeting House to meditate on a text from the
Holy Scriptures.

ARTICLE VI. *The Governor alone is permitted to smoke tobacco.*
But he may do so only on Sunday afternoons during the current
month, once a fortnight in the ensuing month, once only in the
next month, and thereafter only once every other month.
Gloss. *I have only recently discovered the pleasures afforded*
by the late Van Deyssel's china-bowled pipe. Alas, the tobacco
in his jar will last only a very short time. I must prolong

*it as far as possible, and not fall into a habit of which the
deprivation would later cause me discomfort.*

At this point Robinson paused. Closing the Book of the
Charter, he opened another volume, equally unsullied, and
wrote in capital letters on the title page:

PENAL CODE OF THE ISLAND OF SPERANZA, INSTI-
TUTED ON THE 1000TH DAY OF THE LOCAL CALEN-
DAR.

He turned the page, and after careful reflection wrote:

ARTICLE THE FIRST. *Failure to observe the Charter may be visited
with two penalties: fasting and ditchdigging.*
  Gloss. *These are the only penalties capable of being applied,
since corporal punishment and the death penalty require an
increase in the population. The ditch is situated in the stretch
of meadowland between the outcroppings of rock and the first
marshes. It is exposed to the full glare of the sun during the
six hottest hours of the day.*

ARTICLE II. *All wallowing in the mire is strictly forbidden. Those
contravening this order will be punished with a double stint of
ditching.*
  Gloss. *The ditch thus becomes the antithesis and in a sense
the antidote to the mire. This Article subtly illustrates the
principle whereby a wrongdoer shall be punished in the manner
of his misdeed.*

ARTICLE III. *Whosoever pollutes the island with his excrement
shall fast for one day.*
  Gloss. *Another instance of the subtle relation between crime
and punishment.*

ARTICLE IV. . . .

Robinson paused for a moment while he considered suitable penalties for offenses against public morals within the confines of the island and its territorial waters. He went to the door and opened it, as though to show himself to his subjects. The rolling greenery of the tropical forest swept down to the sea, which farther off merged with the sky. Because he was redheaded as a fox, his mother had clad him from childhood in green, teaching him to avoid blue, which, she said, did not suit the ginger of his hair and was inappropriate to his attire. But nothing could have been more harmonious at the moment than that sea of foliage against the background of sea and sky; and the whole scene, sun and sea, forest and empyrean, was fixed in a state so motionless that time itself might have seemed suspended, were it not for the liquid ticking of his clock. "If," Robinson reflected, "there is ever to be a Revelation, a manifestation of the Divine Spirit descending upon me, the legislator of Speranza, it should happen on a day and at a moment such as this. A tongue of flame dancing above my head, or a column of smoke rising like a spear to the zenith—would not these testify that I am the temple of God?"

And as he uttered the words, speaking them aloud in accordance with Article II of the Charter, he saw beyond the curtain of the forest a thin wisp of smoke rising into the sky, apparently from the Bay of Salvation. Thinking at first that it was the answer to his prayer, he fell upon his knees, uttering words of praise. But then a doubt entered his mind. Getting to his feet, he went back into the Residence and equipped himself with his musket, a bag of powder, a pouch of bullets, and the spyglass. He whistled to Tenn and plunged into the undergrowth, avoiding the direct path he had made from the cave to the shore.

About forty dark-skinned men were grouped in a circle around a fire from which a column of thick, milky smoke of unnatural density was now rising. Three long canoes with outriggers had been hauled up onto the beach. They were of the type common throughout the Pacific, remarkable for their seaworthiness despite their narrowness and shallow draft. As for the men, Robinson identified them through his glass as coastal Indians from the fearsome tribe of the Araucanians, inhabiting the central part of Chile, who had held the Inca invaders at bay and inflicted bloody defeats on the Spanish conquistadores. They were short, sturdy men clad only in crude leather aprons. Their broad faces, with remarkably wide-set eyes, were rendered stranger still by their custom of completely plucking their eyebrows, and by the thick, black, gleaming head of beautifully kept hair which they shook proudly on every pretext. Robinson had seen something of them during visits to Temuco, their capital in Chile, and he knew that if another war had broken out between them and the Spanish, no white man could look for mercy at their hands.

Had they come all the way from the coasts of Chile to Speranza? This was by no means impossible, in view of their navigational exploits, but it seemed more likely that they had colonized one of the other Juan Fernández Islands; and it was fortunate for Robinson that chance had not flung him into their midst, since he would probably have been killed at once, or at best enslaved.

Knowing what he did of the customs of their country, he could guess the nature of the ceremony that was now taking place. An emaciated, wild-haired woman, dancing and quivering within the circle of men, drew near the fire, flung a handful of powder into it, and avidly inhaled the dense white fumes that arose. Then, as though intoxicated, she turned toward the motionless circle and began to walk slowly around it, seeming to examine the men and pausing abruptly in front of one or two. She then returned to the fire and again inhaled the smoke, so that Robinson began to wonder whether, witch doctress though she was, she would not collapse from asphyxiation before the ritual was complete. But no: the climax suddenly came. Rising to her full height in her tattered garments, she stretched out her arms toward one of the men, while her wide-opened mouth seemed to cry valedictions that Robinson could not hear. The man thus singled out as responsible for whatever calamity had befallen them, sickness or drought, fell with his face to the ground, trembling violently. One of the others went up to him and with a machete cut away the wretched garment he was wearing. Then the machete descended in a series of regular blows, cutting off the head, arms, and legs. The six sections of the body were cast on the flames, while the witch squatted on the sand either asleep or ill, or perhaps relieving herself, or praying.

The circle broke up and the men took no more interest in the fire, of which the smoke had turned black. They returned to their canoes, and six of them got out water bags and disappeared under the trees. Robinson hastily drew back while still keeping a watchful eye on the invaders of his solitude. If they were to find any trace of his presence they might scour the island in search of him and he would be hard put to escape. Fortunately there was a fresh-water stream nearby, and they had no need to penetrate inland. Carrying the filled water bags slung from poles on their shoulders, the six men returned to the canoes, which the others had refloated. The witch was lying prostrate on a sort of throne erected in the stern of one of them.

When the three craft had vanished beyond the cliffs at the end of the bay, Robinson went down to examine the funeral pyre. The charred remains of the victim were still visible. Thus, he reflected, do primitive peoples, unwittingly and with the cruelty that is natural to them, obey the behest of the Gospel according to St. Matthew: *"Wherefore if thy hand or thy foot offend thee, cut them off and cast them from thee: it is better for thee to enter into life halt or maimed, rather than having two hands or feet to be cast into everlasting fire. And if thine eye offend thee, pluck it out. . . ."* But did not charity join with practical economy in counseling that it was better to dress the gangrened eye, better to purify the member of the community whose error had brought shame upon his fellows?

It was with a mind beset by doubts that the Governor of Speranza returned to his Residence.

ARTICLE VII. *The Island of Speranza is declared a Fortified Place under the command of the Governor, who is hereby accredited with the rank of General. Curfew is obligatory one hour after sunset.*

ARTICLE VIII. *Sunday ceremonial is extended to include working days.*
    Gloss. *Every increase in the pressure of events must be compensated by an equivalent increase in the strictness of behavior. This calls for no elucidation.*

Setting down his vulture's quill, Robinson looked about him. In front of the official Residence, the Pavilion of Weights and Measures, the Palace of Justice, and the Meeting Hall, there was now a crenelated wall made out of the earth excavated from a dry moat twelve feet deep and ten feet wide, running in an ample semicircle from one side of the cave to the other. The two flint muskets and the double-barreled pistol were ready in position in its three central loopholes. In case of an attack Robinson could delude his assailants into believing that he was not the only defender. The boarding cutlass and the ax were also in readiness, although it was unlikely that it would ever come to hand-to-hand fighting, because the approaches to the battlements were thickly sown with snares. First came a number of pits in staggered rows, concealed by tufts of grass or reed matting, each with a sharp wooden spike in the center. In the clearing at the entrance to the footpath leading to the bay, at the point where an enemy force might pause to regroup before making its final advance, Robinson had buried a barrel of gunpowder with a fuse so that it could be exploded at a distance. And finally the bridge over the moat could, of course, be raised from within.

The work of fortification, and his constant fear of a return visit by the Araucanians, had kept Robinson in a state of suspense which was both morally and physically bracing. Once again he found that to build, to organize, and to make and abide by rules were sovereign remedies against the demoralizing effects of solitude. Never had he felt so far removed from the temptations of the mire. Every evening before curfew he went on his round accompanied by Tenn, who seemed to understand the danger that threatened them. The fortress was then "locked up" for the night. Small boulders were rolled into positions calculated to lead possible assailants toward the hidden pits. The drawbridge was raised, all entrances were barricaded, and the curfew was rung. Robinson then prepared his evening meal, laid the table in

the Residence, and withdrew into his cave, to emerge a few
minutes later washed and scented and clad in his coat of
ceremony, with his hair combed and his beard trimmed.
Finally, by the light of a candelabrum holding a bunch of
twigs steeped in resin, he ate his dinner slowly under the
watchful and worshiping eyes of Tenn.

This period of intense warlike activity was followed by a
brief spell of heavy rain which entailed arduous labors of
repair and maintenance, and then it was time for the wheat
and barley harvest. The yield was so heavy that for additional storage room Robinson resorted to a small cave leading
out of the main one, its entrance so narrow that hitherto
he had made no use of it. And now he did not deny himself
the pleasure of breadmaking. He put aside a small part
of his yield, and at last he was able to heat the oven which
he had held in readiness for so long. It was a tremendous
event whose solemnity was by no means lost on him, although not until later did he appreciate its full importance.
Once again he was participating in that most material and
most spiritual of human activities. But if that first baking,
in its mystical and universal significance, took him to the
very roots of mankind, it also harbored in its twofold nature
implications that were peculiar to himself—hidden, intimate,
buried amid the shameful secrets of his early childhood—
which foreshadowed an unforeseen flowering of his solitary
state.

Journal

*Kneading my dough for the first time this morning, I was
visited by memories, long buried under the business of living,*

which my isolation has revived. I was about ten when my father asked me what I wanted to be when I grew up. I replied unhesitatingly, a baker. He looked gravely at me and then nodded with a smile of affectionate approval. There can be no doubt that the humble calling was endowed with a particular dignity in his eyes, hallowed by the symbolism attaching to bread, the first food of the body and also the food of the soul, according to the Christian tradition, which his Quaker upbringing had taught him to reject, even though he held it in respect for its ancient origin.

For me there was something else, although at that time I had no thought of defining the special fascination which the baker's trade held for me. On my way to school in the morning I passed a grating in a wall from which flowed a current of air, warm, maternal, as it were carnal, which had caused me to pause for a long time, peering through the bars, the first time I became aware of it. Surrounding me was the damp gloom of the early morning, the muddy street with the unhappy prospect of school and stern masters at its end. But in that lighted cellar I could see a baker's apprentice, stripped to the waist and covered with flour, plunging his arms to the elbow in a thick, creamy mass of dough. I have always preferred the feel of things to their look. The senses of touch and smell are to me more moving and instructive than those of sight and hearing. I do not think this speaks highly for my spiritual nature, but I humbly confess it. For me color is but a promise of hardness or softness, and shape the token of suppleness or rigidity that I can explore with my hands. I could conceive of nothing more pliable or yielding than that headless body of warm and sensuous matter submitting to the plunging caresses of a half-naked man. I know it now, there lurked in my mind the thought of a strange marriage between the dough and the baker, and I even dreamed of a new kind of yeast which would give the bread a musky savor, like a breath of spring.

Thus for Robinson the strenuous ordering of his island was accompanied by the growth, timid at first, of only half-conscious tendencies. It was as though the framework, fragile but feverishly strengthened, which he built around himself existed only to protect the evolution of a new man, destined eventually to emerge. But Robinson did not yet know this, and he continued to despair at the imperfections of the structure he was creating. Indeed, his observance of the Charter and the Penal Code, the punishments he inflicted on himself, his rigid adherence to a time schedule that left him not a moment's respite, the ceremonial which accompanied all his major actions—this strait jacket of conventions and prescriptions which he resolutely wore to stay upright did not prevent him from being agonizingly conscious of the wild and untamed presence of the tropical world surrounding him, or, within himself, of the steady work of erosion effected by solitude on the soul of a civilized man. Although he might deny himself certain sentiments and certain instinctive inferences, he was constantly assailed by superstitions and perplexities that threatened the stability of the edifice devised for his protection.

Thus he could not prevent himself from attributing a fateful significance to the call of a particular bird whose name he did not know. This bird, always hidden in the trees, invisible but often very close to him, was given to uttering two distinct cries, one of which told unmistakably of happiness, while the other sounded a terrifying note of approaching danger. Robinson had developed a mortal fear of that second call, yet he could not restrain himself from adventuring into the dank, somber regions where the birds seemed to lurk, trembling in advance at their warning of harm.

He was becoming increasingly mistrustful of the evidence of his senses, inclined to dismiss things he thought he had seen or heard because of nagging doubts about some aspect of them. At the same time he ceaselessly repeated his investigations of things which seemed to him improbable or suspect or contradictory. For example, while paddling in his canoe off the southwestern coast of the island, he was struck by the loud clamor of birdcalls and insect buzzings which came to him over the water in successive waves. He went ashore; but as he penetrated the forest he found himself plunged in a silence that filled him with uneasy astonishment. Did it mean that this stirring of wildlife was only to be heard from outside and at a distance, or was it he who had provoked the silence? He got back into the canoe and paddled away. But then he returned to the place and again went ashore, repeating the experiment several times, in weariness and exasperation, unable to find an answer to the riddle.

And there were the dunes of coarse sand in the northeastern corner from which a sort of abysmal lowing sound came, like the groaning of the earth itself, which froze him with horror, if only because of the impossibility of determining its cause. It was true that he seemed to have heard of a hill in Chile called El Bramador (a word which meant the belling of a stag) because when anyone walked on it the shifting of the sand set up a subterranean rumble. But had he really heard that tale or had he unconsciously invented it, simply to calm his fears? He could not be sure,

and with a maniacal obstinacy he strode over those dunes
with his mouth wide open, after the ancient belief of sailors,
so that he might hear the better.

Journal

*It is three o'clock in the morning, and I am wide awake. I
wander along the damp passages of the cave. As a child I
would have died of terror at the sight of those shadowy
walls, the vaulted roofs vanishing into darkness, and at the
sound of a drop of water falling on a stone. Solitude is
strong wine. Intolerable to a child, it offers a harsh intoxication to the man who has learned how to still the fluttering
of his heart. May it not be that Speranza is the fulfillment
of a destiny prescribed for me in my earliest years? We got
to know each other, Solitude and I, during my long, con-
templative walks on the banks of the Ouse, and when I
shut myself away in my father's library with a supply of
candles to last me through the night, and again in London
when I refused to make use of letters of introduction to
friends of our family. When the Virginia ended her career
on the reefs of Speranza I entered solitude as naturally as
one may enter religion after a too devout childhood. Solitude
had awaited me on these shores from the beginning of time,
with its enforced companion, silence. . . .*

*Since I have been here I have become something of a
specialist in silence, or in silences, I should say. With my
whole being intent like a single ear, I note the particular
quality of the silence at a given moment. There are airy,
scented silences like a June night in England, others with
the glaucous thickness of the mire, and yet others that are*

*hard and sonorous as ebony. I find myself plumbing the
tomblike depths of night silence in the cave with a vague,
queasy pleasure that somewhat perturbs me. Even by day
I have nothing to connect me with life—wife, children,
friends, enemies, servants, customers—those anchors that
keep our feet on earth. Why is it that in the heart of darkness
I let myself stray so far, so deeply into the night? It may
well be that presently I shall vanish without trace, sucked
into the nothingness I shall have created around me.*

The store of grain accumulating from year to year gave
rise to serious problems in protecting it against rats. The
number of rats seemed to increase in exact proportion to
the increasing supply of food, and Robinson constantly
marveled at this power of the animal world to adapt itself
to the resources of its environment, unlike the human species,
which multiplies as its wealth diminishes. But since he was
resolved to continue amassing harvest after harvest while
strength remained to him, he had to take drastic measures
against parasites.

There were certain redheaded fungi that seemed to be
poisonous, since several young goats had died after eating
them where they grew in the grass. Robinson made an infusion of these in which he soaked grains of wheat. He scattered
the wheat along the paths followed by the rats, and they
ate them and were none the worse. Then he devised cages
with one-way doors; but he would have needed thousands
of such traps to serve his purpose, and moreover the sight
of those small, intelligent eyes glaring at him in hatred as he
sank the cages in the stream filled him with abhorrence. Solitude had rendered him intensely susceptible to anything re-

sembling hostility to himself, even on the part of the most worthless of vermin. The carapace of indifference and mutual ignorance with which men shield themselves in their relations to one another had slipped from him, like a callus vanishing from an idle hand.

One day he witnessed a mortal combat between two rats. Blind and deaf to everything around them, they rolled over on the ground uttering furious squeaks. In the end each had ripped out the throat of the other, and they died still locked in an embrace. Upon examining the bodies, Robinson found that they belonged to two quite different species. One was black, round, and smooth-skinned, in every way similar to rats he had killed in the ships he had sailed in. The other was gray, longer in the body, and with a thicker coat, a country rat such as he had seen in those parts of the grassland where apparently they lived. There could be no doubt that these were native to the island, whereas the first variety must be the descendants of the survivors from the *Virginia*, now waxing plentiful on the fruits of his harvest. Both varieties appeared to have their own food supplies and their separate domains. Robinson confirmed this one evening by releasing in the grassland a black rat which he had captured in the cave. For a time only the quivering of the grass revealed the progress of an invisible hunt in which numerous small creatures were involved. Then the hunt narrowed, and a cloud of dust arose at the foot of one of the dunes. When Robinson reached the spot he found nothing left of his captive except its skin and bones. Accordingly he made a heap of two sacks of grain in that part of the meadow, and laid a trail from it to the cave. It was a heavy sacrifice that might have been wasted, but was not. That night the black rats came out in force to retrieve what they doubtless held to be their own property. A battle followed, and it was as though a storm had broken out over several acres of the meadow, raising countless small clouds of dust. The warring rats rolled over and over like living balls, while a sound of squealing filled the air as though from some infernal playground. Under the light of a brilliant moon the plain seemed to be boiling in a tumult of infant cries.

The outcome was what might have been expected. The animal which fights on enemy territory is always the loser. That night all the black rats perished.

Journal

Last night my right arm, which was hanging down from my couch, went to sleep, or "died." I took it in my left hand and lifted it up, that lifeless, heavy object of flesh and bone that might have been a part of some other person, attached to me in error. I dream of thus handling my whole body, marveling at the dead weight, lost in the paradox of this thing which is myself. But is it really me? I remember my feeling as a child when, being taken into a church in York, I saw a stained-glass window depicting the martyrdom of St. Denis. The saint had been decapitated on the steps of the Temple, and the headless body bent down and picked up the head in its two big hands. . . . What caused me to marvel was not merely this evidence of prodigious vitality. To me in my infant piety the divine miracle was a commonplace, and besides, I had myself seen a duck running with its head cut off. No, the true marvel was that being deprived of his head, St. Denis had sought for it in the stream into which it had rolled, and that he had picked it up so carefully, with such affectionate solicitude. If it were I who had been beheaded I would certainly not have gone running after that unsightly object whose red hair and freckles were the bane of my life! How bitterly I deplored them, my flaming head of hair, long, skinny arms, legs like stilts, and white body like that of a plucked goose with here and there a fluff of pinkish down. My hearty dislike of all this gave me a view of myself which has only achieved its fullness on Speranza. For some time indeed I have been performing an act of surgery on myself which consists of stripping away in turn all my attributes—I say all—like peeling an onion. And at the same time I am constructing, separate from myself, a man called Crusoe, Christian name Robinson, six feet tall, etc. . . . and I watch him live and grow on this island, without participating in his good fortune or suffering from his bad luck. What "I" is this? The question is far from an idle one, nor is it even unanswerable. Because if it is not him then it must be Speranza. There is a fluttering "I" which comes to rest now on the man and now on the island, making of me one and the other by turns.

Is this not what is called "philosophy," this that I have just written? What strange transformation is taking place within me that I, the most positive and least speculative of men, should be not only putting such questions to myself but, as it would seem, answering them! I must return to this matter.

His dislike of his own face, and an upbringing opposed to all personal vanity, had caused Robinson to avoid the mirror he had brought from the *Virginia*, which he had hung on the least accessible part of the outside wall of the

Residence. But his interest in the change he was undergoing drew him to it one morning, and he even brought out his chair so that he could examine more closely the only human face it was given to him to observe.

Although there was no marked alteration in his features, he scarcely recognized himself. A single word occurred to him —disfigured. "I am disfigured," he said aloud, while despair clutched his heart. Vainly he searched, in the tightness of the mouth, the lackluster eyes, the characterlessness of the forehead—faults with which he had always been familiar—for something to account for the shadowy distortion of the mask that gazed back at him through the damp-stains in the mirror. The cause lay in something wider and deeper, a kind of hardness, a hint of death such as he had once seen in the face of a prisoner set free after years of captivity in a lightless dungeon. It was as though a winter of pitiless severity had passed over that familiar countenance, ridding it of all light and shade, congealing its mobility, simplifying its expression to the point of coarseness. Indeed, the square beard which framed it from one ear to the other had none of the flowing softness of the beard of the man from Nazareth! It belonged rather to the Old Testament, with its summary justice, as did that overdirect gaze, alarming in its Mosaic harshness.

Like a new kind of Narcissus, plunged in distress and filled with renewed self-distaste, Robinson spent a long time communing with his reflected self. He realized that the face is the part of our flesh which is endlessly molded and remolded, warmed, animated by the presence of our fellows. After parting from someone with whom he has had an animated conversation, a man's face retains a glow which only gradually fades and may be rekindled if he meets some-

one else. "An expressionless face. A degree of extinction such
as perhaps no human being has ever before undergone."
Robinson spoke these words too aloud, but his face as he
did so betrayed no more emotion than if his voice had issued
from some brass instrument. In an attempt at gaiety he
sought to smile, but could not. There was in truth something
frozen in his face, and only a long and happy reunion with
his own kind could have caused it to thaw. Only a friend's
smile could have given him back his own.

Tearing himself away from the horrid fascination of the
mirror, he gazed about him. Did he not possess everything
he needed on this island? He could quench his thirst and appease his hunger, provide for his safety and even for his
comfort, and the Bible was there to satisfy his spiritual needs.
But who, by the simple power of a smile, would ever melt
the ice that froze his countenance? He looked down at Tenn,
who was seated on the ground at his side, gazing up at him.
Was he dreaming? *Tenn was smiling at his master.* The
black, finely serrated lip was curled back on one side of his
mouth, disclosing a double row of fangs, while his head was
comically inclined to one side and his nut-brown eyes
seemed to be wrinkled in laughter. Robinson took the shaggy
head between his hands, while his own eyes grew misty
with tenderness. A forgotten warmth tinged his cheeks, and
he felt an unfamiliar tremor at the corners of his mouth—
as when, on the banks of the Ouse, the first breath of March
had heralded the approaching stir of spring. Tenn was still
smiling, and Robinson peered intently at him, seeking to recover that sweetest of human faculties. Thereafter it was
like a game between them. Robinson would abruptly stop
whatever he was doing—or even light a torch in the middle
of the night—and, with a face now only half dead, gaze at

Tenn in a particular fashion. And Tenn would smile at him with his head on one side, and his dog's smile would be reflected ever more clearly on the face of the man, his master.

There was a glow of pink in the dawn sky, but the grand concert of birds and insects had not yet begun. Not a breath of wind stirred the palms decorating either side of the open door of the Residence. Robinson had awakened much later than usual. He realized this at once, but, no doubt because his conscience was still asleep, he did not rebuke himself. He lay picturing in his mind the day that awaited him beyond the door. First his toilet, then the reading of a passage of the Bible at the lectern, then the saluting of the colors and the formal opening of his citadel. He would let down the drawbridge, and shift the boulders blocking the way to it. His morning would be devoted to his livestock. The she-goats numbered B_{13}, L_{24}, G_2, and Z_{17} must be taken to be serviced by males. With a certain disgust Robinson pictured their indecent haste as he led them, skinny legs quivering and dugs flapping, to the male enclosure. He would leave them there all the morning to fornicate as they pleased. Then he must visit the artificial rabbit warren he was seeking to establish. It was a sandy hollow, overgrown with gorse and broom, around which he had built a low dry-stone wall, tilling within it small crops of turnips, lucerne, and oats, in the hope of persuading a colony of agoutis to settle there—a variety of short-eared golden hare, of which he had been able to kill very few since he had been on Speranza. Also he must find time before lunch to raise the water level in his three fresh-water fishponds, which were beginning to feel the drought. After this he would have a snack and then change into his general's uniform, because that afternoon he had to perform a series of official functions: announce the result of the census of sea turtles, take the chair at the Drafting Committee of the Charter and Penal Code, and finally preside at the opening of a new bridge of lianas flung audaciously across a ravine a hundred feet deep in the heart of the forest.

He lay wondering whether in addition to all this he would find time to complete the summerhouse of tree fern he had begun to build at the edge of the forest overlooking the bay, which was to serve not only as a lookout post commanding an excellent view of the sea, but also as a cool retreat in the heat of the day: and suddenly he realized why it was that he had awakened so late. He had forgotten to fill his water clock the night before, and it had run dry. Indeed, it was the falling of the last drop into the copper bowl that drew his attention to the unaccustomed silence. Turning to look at it, he saw that the drop that should have followed was clinging uncertainly to the bottom of the glass jar; it stretched till it was pear-shaped, hesitated, and then, as though discouraged, resumed its spherical shape; and finally it returned whence it had come, not merely refusing to fall, but seeming to reverse the passage of time.

Robinson stretched luxuriously on his couch. This was the first occasion for months that the inexorable dripping had not dictated his every movement as rigorously as if it had been a conductor's baton. Time had stopped, and he was on holiday! He sat on the edge of the couch, and Tenn came and laid his muzzle on his knee. So it seemed that Robinson's omnipotence over the island, born of his solitude, extended even to the mastery of time! He reflected with delight that he had only to plug the hole in the water clock and he could suspend the passing of time whenever he chose!

He got up and stood in the doorway. He was trembling from his state of happy astonishment, and had to lean his shoulder against the doorpost. Later, reflecting on that wave of ecstasy and seeking to put a name to it, he called it a "moment of innocence." He had thought at first that the stopping of the clock had done no more than interfere with the routine of his day and make it appear less urgent; but now he perceived that the pause was less his affair than that of the island as a whole. It was as though in ceasing to be related to each other according to their use—and their abuse —things had returned to their own essence, were flowering in their own right and existing simply for their own sakes, seeking no other warrant than their own fulfillment. A great tenderness filled the heavens, as though God, in a sudden outpouring of love, were resolved to bless all His creation. There was a radiance in the air; and in a moment of inexpressible happiness Robinson seemed to discern *another island* behind the one where he had labored so long in solitude, a place more alive, warmer and more fraternal, which his mundane preoccupations had concealed from him.

This was a wonderful discovery. It seemed after all that it was possible to escape from the relentless discipline of the work schedule and the ceremonial, without of necessity returning to the mire. Change was possible without decay! He could break the equilibrium so laboriously acquired and raise himself yet higher, instead of falling back. Unquestionably he had advanced another step in the transformation that was at work deep within him. But all this was no more than a flash of revelation. In a moment of ecstasy the larva had learned that one day it would fly. Intoxicating but fleeting vision!

Thereafter he frequently stopped the clock, to pursue experiments which one day, perhaps, would cause the new Robinson to emerge from the chrysalis wherein he still slumbered. But the time had not yet come. The *other island* did not show itself again in the rosy mist of dawn, as it had on that memorable morning. Patiently he resumed his customary garments and went on with the game where he had left off, forgetting in the routine of small tasks and ceremonies that for a moment he had dreamed of other things.

Journal

I am not versed in philosophy, but the long periods of meditation to which I am inescapably reduced, and above all the crumbling, as it were, of certain of my mental faculties, owing to the lack of human society, have led me to certain conclusions regarding the ancient riddle of consciousness. It seems to me, in a word, that the presence of others—and their unregarded intrusion into all our thinking—is a serious cause of confusion and obscurity in the relationship between the knower and the known. This does not mean that others do not have an essential part to play in that relationship, but that it should take place at the proper time and in the light of day, not at inappropriate moments and as it were by stealth.

A candle carried in a darkened room throws its light on particular objects while leaving the rest in darkness. Things emerge for a moment into light and then return to shadow. But whether or not the light has caught them they do not change, either in their nature or in the fact of their existence.

Such as they were before the light fell upon them, such are they during and after its passing.

This is our customary image, more or less, of the act of knowledge, the candle representing the knower and the lighted object the known. But what solitude has taught me is this: that this precept is concerned with the knowledge of things by others, *that is to say, with a particular and narrow aspect of the problem of knowledge. A stranger entering any house who notices certain things, then turns to look at others—this corresponds precisely to the image of the candle moving through a darkened room. But the problem of knowledge as a whole must be defined at an earlier and more fundamental stage: for if I am to talk of a stranger entering my house and noting the things he finds there, I must myself be there, seeing the room and observing the conduct of the stranger.*

Thus there are two problems of knowledge, or rather two kinds of knowledge, between which a sharp distinction must be made, but which I should doubtless have gone on confusing had not my present fate induced in me an entirely new view of things: there is knowledge through others *and knowledge* through oneself. *To confound the two on the assumption that "the other" is another self is to get nowhere. Yet this is what we do when we depict the knower as any individual entering a room and seeing, touching, smelling— in a word, knowing—the objects he finds there. That individual is "the other," but the things he sees are known to* me, *the observer of the scene. If therefore the problem is to be correctly stated, I must depict the situation, not of another person entering the room, but of myself, speaking and seeing. Which I will now attempt to do.*

A first point that must be noted, in attempting to depict

the self *unrelated to others, is that it exists only intermittently and, when all is said, comparatively seldom. Its presence corresponds to a secondary and as it were reflexive mode of knowledge. What happens in the primary, direct mode? Well, the objects are all there, shining in the sun or buried in the shade, rough or smooth, light or heavy; they are known, tested, touched, even cooked, carved, folded, and so on; whereas I who do the knowing, the tasting, touching, and cooking, have no separate existence except when I perform the act of reflection which causes* me *to emerge—a thing which in fact rarely happens. In that primary state of knowledge my awareness of an object is the object itself, the thing known and perceived without any person knowing and perceiving it. We cannot use the image of the candle shedding its light upon objects. We must substitute another: that of objects shining unaided, with a light of their own.*

In that innocent, primary—as it were, primeval—stage which is our normal mode of existence there is a happy solitude of the known, a virginity of things comprising all things in themselves like so many functions of their own essence—color, smell, taste, and form. In this sense Robinson is Speranza. He is conscious of himself only in the stir of myrtle leaves with the sun's rays breaking through, he knows himself only in the white crest of a wave running up the yellow sand.

Then suddenly there is a click. The subject breaks away from the object, divesting it of a part of its color and substance. There is a rift in the scheme of things, and a whole range of objects crumbles in becoming me, *each object transferring its quality to an appropriate subject. The light becomes the eye and as such no longer exists: it is* simply the stimulation of the retina. The smell becomes the nostril—and the world declares itself odorless. The song of the wind in the trees is disavowed: it was nothing but a quivering of the timpani. Until finally the whole world has been absorbed into my soul, which is the soul of Speranza, plucked out of the island, which then dies beneath my skeptical gaze.

An upheaval has taken place. Object has been roughly degraded to subject. No doubt it deserved to be, since this whole mechanism has a purpose. A knot of contradiction, a center of discord, it has been eliminated from the body of the island, rejected, repudiated. The click represents a process which is the rationalization of the world. The world seeks its own reason and in doing so casts off that irrelevance, the subject.

One day a Spanish galleon came sailing toward Speranza. Nothing could have seemed more real. But it is more than a century since the last galleon vanished from the seas. And a feast was being held on board. But instead of anchoring and lowering a boat, the ship sailed past as though the shore were a thousand miles away. And a girl in old-fashioned clothes looked at me from a cabin window, and she was my sister, dead two decades ago. So many implausibilities were not acceptable. The click happened, and the galleon was stripped of its pretension to exist. It became Robinson's hallucination, absorbed into the subject, a haggard Robinson suffering from brain fever.

One day while walking in the forest, I saw a tree stump in my path, fifty yards away. A strange tree stump, hairy one would have said, looking something like an animal. And the stump moved. But this was impossible—tree stumps do not move! And then it turned into a goat. But how could a tree stump turn into a goat? The click was necessary, and it occurred. The stump vanished, not only in the present but in the past. There had never been a stump but only a goat. The stump was an illusion born of Robinson's defective eyesight.

The subject is the disqualified object. My eye is the corpse of light and color. My nose is all that remains of odors when their unreality has been demonstrated. My hand refutes the thing it holds. Thus the problem of awareness is born of anachronism. It implies the simultaneous existence of the subject with the object, whose mysterious relationship to himself he seeks to define. But subject and object cannot exist apart from one another since they are one and the same thing, at first integrated into the real world and then cast out by it. Robinson is the excrement of Speranza.

This prickly formula gives me a somber satisfaction. It shows me the rough and narrow road to salvation, at least to a kind of salvation—that of a fruitful and harmonious island, flawlessly cultivated and administered, strong in the harmony of all its attributes, steadily pursuing its course without me, because it is so close to me that even to look at it is to make it too much myself, so that I must shrink to become that intimate phosphorescence which causes each thing to be known while no one is the knower, each to be aware while no one has awareness. . . . Oh, subtle and pure equilibrium, so fragile and so precious!

But Robinson was impatient to dismiss these dreams and speculations and tread the firm soil of Speranza. A day dawned when he believed he had found a real road leading to the most secret intimacy of the island.

CHAPTER FIVE

Situated at the center of the island near the giant cedar tree, like a great air vent at the base of the mass of rock, the cavern had always been of fundamental importance to Robinson, although for a long time he had used it only as a storehouse for his hoarded wealth: the growing stocks of grain, preserved fruit, and salted meat; the tools and weapons, the chests of clothes and box of gold; finally, right at the back, the barrels of black powder which would have been sufficient to blow up the whole island. Although he had long ceased to use firearms for hunting, Robinson attached great value to that stored destructive force, capable of being released whenever he chose, and to the sense of mastery it gave him. Armed like Jove with thunderbolts, he asserted his power of life and death over the island and its inhabitants.

But now the cave had assumed a new significance for him. In his new life—the life which began when, putting aside his functions as governor, military commander, and administrator, he stopped the water clock—Speranza was no longer a territory to be exploited, but a being, unquestionably feminine, toward whom he directed not only his philosophical speculations, but also the new needs arising in his heart and flesh. He began to wonder confusedly whether the cave might not be the mouth or eye or some other orifice of that great body, and whether in exploring its whole extent he might not discover some hidden recess corresponding to the questions which were now stirring in his mind.

Beyond the powder magazine was a narrow tunnel inclining steeply downward which he had never explored until he entered what he was later to call the earth-bound phase of his life. One reason was that the enterprise raised a problem of particular difficulty, that of lighting.

To venture into those depths carrying a torch of resinous twigs, and he had nothing else, was to run a serious risk from the proximity of the powder barrels, for he could never be sure that some part of the contents had not spilled on the ground. It also meant that the motionless, rarefied air of the cave would be filled with dense, unbreathable fumes. After considering and dismissing the idea of driving a light-and-ventilation shaft from the surface to the far end of the cave, he found that he had no alternative but to accept the fact of darkness, to adapt himself to the exigencies of the new realm he sought to conquer; a thought which would certainly not have occurred to him a few weeks previously. But being aware now of the transformation he was undergoing, he was prepared to subject himself to the most vigorous discipline for the sake of what might turn out to be a new way of life.

At first he made tentative efforts to accustom himself to darkness by feeling his way around the remoter parts of the cave. But he realized that this was not enough, and that a more drastic course of preparation was needed. He must go beyond the state of light or dark in which man normally lives, into the true world of the blind, which is complete and flawless, certainly less convenient to live in than the world of sight, yet not wholly divorced from light or plunged in unrelieved darkness, as those with eyes suppose. The eye which invented light also invented darkness; those without eyes are ignorant of both, but they do not suffer from the absence of the former. The only way of attaining this state was to spend a very long time in total darkness, and this was what Robinson did, surrounded by wheat cakes and jugs of goats' milk.

Around him absolute quiet prevailed. Not a sound penetrated the depths of the cave. Yet he already knew that the experiment was destined to succeed, because he found that he was in no way cut off from Speranza. On the contrary, he lived intensely with her. Seated with his back to the rocky wall, his eyes wide open in the darkness, he saw the white unfolding of the sea on all the shores of the island, the benevolent sway of palm leaves stirred by the wind, the red flash of a hummingbird against a green sky. He smelled the moist freshness of the sand uncovered by the ebb, and watched a hermit crab as it took the air at the doorway of its shell. A black-headed gull slowed suddenly in its flight to swoop down upon a small creature half-hidden in red seaweed, gleaming brown in the drag of the undertow. Robinson's sense of solitude was dispelled in a strange fashion, not sidelong by winks and nudges, as when one is with a friend in a crowd, but centrally, as it were from the nucleus itself. He felt that he was near the core of Speranza, the beating heart, the mind from which her nerve ends ran to all the parts of that great body, and into which flowed all intelligence coming from the surface: just as in some cathedrals there is a central point where because of the play of sound waves and vibrations one can hear the smallest sound, whether it comes from the transept or the nave, the reredos or the choir.

The sun must be sinking toward the horizon. At the foot of the rocky pile which crowned the island the cave opened its black mouth like a round, astonished eye gazing over the sea. In a little while the sun would come level with it. Would the end of the cave be lighted by its rays? And for how long? Robinson was soon to learn, and, without being able to explain it, he attached great importance to the discovery.

The event, when it happened, was over so quickly that he wondered if it had been an optical illusion, a phosphorescent gleam in his own eyes, or even a lightning flash which had pierced the darkness without harming him. He had expected something like the raising of a curtain, a triumphant dawn, but it had been no more than a pin point of light in the black intensity that encompassed him. The tunnel must be either longer or more winding than he had thought. But what did this matter? The two eyes had met, the gaze of light and the gaze of darkness. A solar arrow had pierced the earthy soul of Speranza.

The next day the same thing happened. Time passed. The darkness persisted, although it no longer afflicted him with that slight vertigo which causes the walker deprived of visible points of reference to stumble. He was in the belly of Speranza like a fish in water, but still he had not attained that point beyond light and darkness which he felt to be the threshold of an absolute Beyond. Perhaps he should undertake a course of purification by fasting? In any case he had only a little milk left. He stayed where he was for another twenty-four hours, then got to his feet and, without hesitation or fear, but filled with a profound sense of the solemnity of the occasion, started toward the end of the tunnel. He had not gone far before he found what he was seeking, the mouth of a narrow vertical chimney. He made several un-successful attempts to slide down it. Although the walls were smooth as human flesh the opening was so small that his hips would not pass. Accordingly he stripped, and after rubbing his body with the remains of the milk, went headfirst into the bottleneck, and this time slid down slowly but steadily like food down a human gullet. After a very gentle descent which might have lasted for seconds or for centuries, he landed on his outstretched arms in a sort of narrow crypt, its ceiling so low that he could stand upright in it only by thrusting his head into the opening by which he had en-tered. He explored it carefully with his hands. The floor was firm, smooth, and strangely warm, but the walls pre-sented astonishing irregularities. There were stony nipples and protuberances, mineral mushrooms, petrified sponges. Further on, the surface was covered with a tapestry of curled papillae which became rougher and thicker as he drew near a big mineral flower, a sort of limestone concretion, not un-like the sand roses that can be found in some deserts. A damp metallic smell emanated from this, comforting in its acidity, with a trace of sugared tartness recalling the sap of a fig tree. But what attracted Robinson more than anything else was a cavity or recess about five feet deep, which he found in the furthest corner of the crypt. Its walls were perfectly smooth but curiously shaped, like the inside of a mold con-structed for some very complex object. The object, Robin-son suspected, was his own body, and after a number of attempts he succeeded in finding a posture—knees drawn up to his chin, shins crossed, hands resting on his feet—which enabled him to fit so exactly into the recess that he forgot the limitations of his body as soon as he had adopted it.

He was suspended in a happy eternity. Speranza was a

fruit ripening in the sun whose white and naked seed, embedded in a thousand thicknesses of skin and husk and rind, bore the name of Robinson. How describe his sense of peace, installed in this most secret place, in the rocky intimacy of the unknown island? Had there ever before been a shipwreck on its shores, and a survivor of that shipwreck who, turning laborer and administrator, had covered its surface with crops and increased the herds in its fields? Or were these exploits no more than the dream without substance of this small, soft grub, buried for eternity within that huge vessel of stone? What was he, if not the very soul of Speranza? He recalled the wooden dolls of his childhood enclosed one within the other, each one hollow, and squeaking when he unscrewed it, except the last and smallest of all, which was solid and unbreakable, the nut, the reason for all the others.

Perhaps he slept. He could not have said. In the state of non-existence in which he found himself the difference between waking and sleeping was barely noticeable. When he racked his brains trying to determine how much time had passed since his entry into the cave, the picture of the stopped water clock confronted him with monotonous persistency. He noted one more occurrence of the flash of light denoting the passage of the sun across the axis of the cave, and it was shortly after this that an event occurred which surprised him, although he had long been expecting something of the kind. The darkness suddenly changed its nature. The blackness in which he was enveloped turned to white. He was floating in white shadow, like a lump of cream in a bowl of milk. And had he not been forced to rub his body with milk in order to penetrate to this depth?

In this deep place the feminine nature of Speranza became wholly maternal, and because the weakening of the bounds of time and space enabled Robinson to plunge as never before into the forgotten world of his childhood, he was haunted by the memory of his mother. He seemed to be clasped in her arms, a strong, high-souled woman, but deeply reserved and not given to the display of sentiment. He could not recall her ever kissing his five brothers and sisters or himself. Yet she was by no means a monster of coldness, and indeed, in all matters not affecting her children, she was the most ordinary of women. He had seen her weep with joy at recovering a family heirloom which for months had been lost. He had seen her beside herself with grief when their father was struck down by a heart attack. But where her children were concerned she was a woman inspired, in the highest sense of the word. Being wholly devoted, like their father, to the Quaker form of belief, she denied the authority of Holy Writ no less than that of the Roman Church. To the outrage of her neighbors she regarded the Bible as a book which, though doubtless inspired by God, had been written and rewritten by human hands and grossly distorted by the vicissitudes of time and history. How much purer and more vital than those faded texts, handed down through the centuries, was the spring of wisdom that she felt within herself! In it God spoke directly to his servant, and the Holy Spirit visited her with its divine light. Her duty as a mother was for her a natural part of this serene faith. In her dealings with her children there was a quality of infallibility that sustained them more than any display of affection could have. She never kissed them, but they read in her eyes that she knew everything about them, feeling their joys and sorrows even more acutely than they did themselves, and that in humbly serving them she drew upon an inexhaustible store of love, clear-sightedness, and courage. The children were dismayed, when they visited neighbors, by the alternation of fury and fondness, cuffs and caresses, which the scolding, overworked women lavished on their offspring, whereas their own mother, always mistress of herself, imperturbably found the right word or gesture to soothe or rejoice their hearts.

One day when their father was away from the house, fire had broken out in the shop on the ground floor. Their mother was with the children on the floor above. The fire had spread through the centuries-old wooden building with a terrifying rapidity. Robinson was then only a few weeks old, his oldest sister perhaps nine years. The cloth merchant, hurriedly returning home, was on his knees in the street, praying that his family had somehow escaped, when he saw his wife emerge calmly from the torrent of flames and smoke: like a tree bowed under the weight of its fruit, she was carrying her six uninjured children—in her arms, on her shoulders, on her back, and clinging to her apron. It was thus that Robinson recalled his mother, a pillar of truth and goodness, a haven of comfort and strength, the refuge of his griefs and fears. And here in this rocky cavity he had rediscovered something of that flawless, dry tenderness, that unfailing, undemonstrative solicitude. He saw again his mother's hands, big hands which neither fondled nor dealt blows, so strong, so sure, so shapely that they were like two angels, fraternal angels working together at the dictates of the spirit. He saw them kneading a paste of smooth, white dough, for it was the eve of Epiphany. Tomorrow the chil-

dren would have a cake of special flour with beans concealed within its folds. He himself was that supple dough,
caught in a hand of all-powerful stone. He was the bean,
caught in the massive, indestructible flesh of Speranza.

The lightning flash penetrated again down into the depths
where he hung suspended, even more disembodied by fasting.
But in the white darkness that enveloped him its effect
seemed reversed: for a fraction of a second the white turned
black, then instantly regained its snowy purity. It was as
though a wave of ink had flowed into the cave, receding
instantly, leaving no trace behind.

Robinson knew that he must break this spell if he ever
wanted to see daylight again. Life and death were so close
to one another in this luminous place that with only a moment of inattention, of relaxation in his will to live, he
could slip from one into the other. He crawled out of the
recess. He was neither paralyzed nor weakened, but lightened, rather, and as it were spiritualized. He climbed without
difficulty up the chimney, in which he now had room to
spare. Having reached the end of the cave, he felt for his
clothes and rolled them in a bundle under his arm without
bothering to dress. The milky obscurity still surrounded him,
and this made him apprehensive. Had he lost his sight during
his long sojourn underground? He was cautiously approaching the entrance when a sword of fire suddenly struck him.
A searing pain assailed his eyes and he covered his face with
his hands.

The midday sun was making the air quiver above the
rocks. It was the hour when even the lizards look for shade.
Robinson walked on, bent double, shivering with cold and
pressing his thighs together, caked with curdled milk. His

helpless exposure to the brambles and sharp pebbles filled him with alarm and shame. He was naked and white. His skin was goose-fleshed like that of a frightened hedgehog that has lost its prickles. His penis had shrunk to nothing. From behind his fingers came a shrill, whimpering sound, like the squeak of a mouse.

He made his way as best he could to the Residence, guided by Tenn, who danced around him in delight at his return, but dismayed by his altered aspect. In the healing half-light of the house his first act was to start the water clock again.

Journal

I am still far from being able to assess the value of my retreat in the heart of Speranza. Was it profit or loss? The answer would call for a long process of inquiry, for which the essential pieces are lacking. It must be said that the recollection of the mire causes me anxiety, since between it and the cave there is an undeniable affinity. But has not the evil thing always aped the good? Lucifer imitates God after his own fashion, which is a grimace. Is the cave a new and more alluring aspect of the mire, or is it its refutation? What is certain is that, like the mire, it recalls to my mind the ghosts of my past, and this retrospective dreaming is in no way appropriate to the daily struggle with which I seek to bring Speranza to the highest possible state of civilization. But whereas the mire principally evoked the memory of my sister Lucy, a passing, tender fancy—morbid, in a word —the cave brings back the lofty and stern figure of my mother. A noble visitation! It is almost as if that great spirit,

*trying to aid the most imperiled of her children, has found
no better way than to incarnate herself in Speranza, so as to
sustain and nurture me. Certainly it was a harsh ordeal, the
return to daylight, even more than the burial in darkness.
Yet in this beneficent discipline I seem to perceive the hand
of my mother, to whom it was a matter of course that
every achievement must be preceded, and in a sense paid for,
by an arduous effort. And how I have been comforted by
that period of retreat! My life now rests on a wonderfully
solid basis; it is rooted in the very heart of the rock, directly
in touch with the forces slumbering within it. Previously
there had always been something insecure in me, an im-
balance that was a source of mental sickness and distress. I
sought to console myself with visions of a house, the house
in which I would end my days, built out of massive blocks
of granite, resting on unshakable foundations. I indulge no
longer in that dream. I no longer need it.*

*It is written that we cannot enter the Kingdom of Heaven
except with the humility of a child. Never was any word of
the Scriptures more literally true. The cave not only affords
me the unshakable rock on which I may rest my poor life;
it is a return to the lost innocence which all men secretly
mourn. It unites as by a miracle the peace of the sweet
maternal darkness and the peace of the grave, the one before,
the other after life.*

Robinson made several more retreats into the cave, but
then was distracted by the needs of the hay and cereal
harvest. Both were so scanty that he was alarmed. Although
neither his personal provisioning nor that of his herds was in

danger, since the island was sufficiently cultivated to sustain
a much larger population, he felt that something in his subtle
relationship with Speranza was out of balance. It seemed to
him that the new strength swelling his muscles, the spring-
tide lightness of heart that caused him to break into a hymn
of praise each morning when he rose, the renewed youth
which he drew from the depths of the cave, were stolen
from Speranza's own source of life and had dangerously
diminished her most secret strength. The generous rains
which ordinarily restored the earth after the heavy labor of
the harvest were this year withheld in a leaden sky, shot
with lightning flashes and always lowering, but unyielding
and dry. A plot of purslane which normally yielded a big
supply of rich, juicy salad this year dried up without ripening.
Several of the she-goats gave birth to stillborn kids. One
day, as a herd of wild pigs crossed the marshland on the
eastern coast, Robinson saw a cloud of dust rising above
them, from which he concluded with profound satisfaction
that the mire must have disappeared. But on the other hand
the two springs from which he was accustomed to draw
fresh water had dried up, and he had to go a long way into
the forest to find another source.

The new spring trickled weakly from a breast of earth
rising in a clearing in the trees, where the island seemed to
have drawn aside her garment of forest. Robinson ran to it
with a sense of wild rejoicing, and as he knelt down to suck
the life-giving draught the words of Moses seemed to glow
beneath his closed lids in letters of flame—"Children of
Israel, I will lead you into a land flowing with milk and
honey."

But he could not conceal from himself the fact that although his own belly might be filled with milk and honey, Speranza herself was being exhausted by the monstrous maternal role he had imposed on her.

Journal

The matter is settled. Yesterday I again went down into the recess. It was the last time, for now I recognize my error. During the night, while I hung suspended in a half sleep, my semen escaped me. I had only time to place my hand, for its protection, over the narrow crevice, no more than two fingers broad, at the very bottom of the womb of Speranza. The words of the Evangelist returned to me, but this time with a warning note: "Except ye become as little children . . ." By what aberration did I pride myself on possessing the innocence of a child? I am a man in the fullness of life and I should accept the role of manhood. The strength I drew from the womb of Speranza was the perilous price of a regression into the sources of myself. It is true that I there found peace and happiness, but with my man's weight I was crushing the earth that nurtured me. Being pregnant with myself, Speranza could no longer conceive, just as the menstrual flow dries up in a prospective mother. Even worse, I came near to sullying her with my semen. What hideous ripening might not that living seed have produced, in the dark, vast warmth of the cave? I think of Speranza swelling like a loaf in which the yeast is working, her bloated body spreading over the surface of the waters, eventually to die in disgorging some monster of incest!

At the peril of my soul, my life, and the integrity of

Speranza, I have explored the intimate ways of this maternal earth. Perhaps later, when age has sterilized my body and sapped my virility, I may go down again into the recess. If I do so I will never re-emerge. Thus I will have given to my remains the most loving and maternal of tombs.

The water clock resumed its steady dripping, and Robinson's tireless activities again filled the earth and sky of Speranza. He was carrying out a project which he had shirked before, thinking it too vast for him to undertake: the conversion of the marshlands on the east coast of the island into rice paddies. He had not touched the sack of rice since he brought it from the *Virginia.* To have consumed it without seeking to multiply it, squander in momentary self-indulgence the capital that might yield a hundred harvests, this to him was a crime—the crime of crimes—which he could not bring himself to commit, which indeed he would have been physically incapable of committing, for not a grain of the slaughtered seed would have passed his lips or been digested by his outraged stomach.

But the cultivation of rice required that the paddy field should be flooded and drained as required, which called for a system of collecting pools, dams, ditches, and sluices. It was a huge undertaking for a single man already burdened with other crops, livestock, and official duties. For months the dripping of the water clock never ceased, but Robinson's regularly kept journal testified to the progress of those meditations on life, death, and sex which were no more than the surface reflection of a metamorphosis in the depths of his being.

Journal

I know now that if the society of others is a fundamental element in the constitution of the human individual, it is nevertheless not irreplaceable. Necessary, yes; but not indispensable, as the Friends of George Fox said with humility of themselves. A man deprived of the companionship of his fellows may replace this companionship out of his own resources. To replace the given *by the* created *is a universal problem, and most especially a human problem if it be true that what sets man apart from the animals is his need to supply by his own efforts those things which Nature bestows gratuitously on the beasts of the field—clothing, weapons, daily nourishment. Alone on my island I could sink to the level of the animals by creating nothing—which, indeed, is what I did at the outset—or become a kind of superman by creating the more because society gives me nothing. Therefore I have built, and I shall continue to build; but the truth is that my work proceeds on two different levels, and in opposite directions. For if on the surface of the island I pursue the work of civilization—tillage, stockbreeding, building, administering, lawgiving—which follows the pattern of human society and is therefore in a sense retrospective, I feel that in myself I am the scene of a more radical process of creation, one which is engaged in finding new and original substitutes for the ruins that solitude has left with me, all more or less tentative and so to speak experimental, but bearing less and less resemblance to the human model from which they sprang. It seems to me impossible that the growing divergence between these two opposed principles can* continue indefinitely. Inevitably a time will come when an increasingly dehumanized Robinson will be incapable of being the governor and architect of an increasingly humanized estate. Already I am conscious of blank periods in my everyday activities. I find myself working without any real belief in what I am doing, and yet the quality and quantity of my work does not suffer from this. On the contrary, there are kinds of repetitive work which have everything to gain from absence of mind: we work for the sake of working, forgetting the end in view. But one cannot continue to hollow out a structure from within indefinitely, without its finally collapsing. The time must surely come when my ordered and cultivated island will wholly cease to interest me. It will then have lost its sole inhabitant.

Why then do I delay? Why not decide now that the time has come? Why? Because in the present state of my soul this would inexorably lead to my return to the mire. A world is being conceived within me. But a world in gestation is another name for chaos. Against this chaos the ordered island —ordered more and more rigorously because in this matter one cannot hold one's ground except by going forward— is my only safeguard, my only refuge. It has saved me and continues to do so every day. Meanwhile my inner world may continue in search of itself. Parts of the chaos are provisionally resolved. For example, I thought that in the cave I had found a workable solution. It was an error, but the experiment was useful. There will be others. I do not know where this progressive re-creation of myself will eventually take me. If I knew, it would mean that the process was ended, final, and complete.

Thus with sexual desire. It is a torrent which Nature and Society have confined within a millrace, a mill, a mechanism *designed to serve an end of which it is not aware, the perpetuation of the species.*

I have lost this outlet. As the social structure within me has crumbled to ruins over the years, so also has perished the framework of institutions and myths that permits desire to become embodied, in the twofold sense of the word—that is to say, to assume a positive form and to expend itself in the body of a woman. To say that my sexual desire is no longer directed toward the perpetuation of the species is not enough. It no longer knows what its purpose is! For a long time memory was sufficiently active in me to feed my imagination with objects of desire, non-existent though they were. But that is over now. Memory has been sucked dry. The creatures of my imagination are lifeless shadows. I may speak the words, woman, breasts, thighs, thighs parted at my desire, but they mean nothing. Words have lost their power; they are sounds, no more. Does this mean that desire has died in me for lack of use? Far from it! I still feel within me that murmur of the spring of life, but it has become objectless. Instead of flowing submissively along the course set for it by society, it floods out in all directions like the rays of a star, as though in search of a channel, the course wherein all the waters will be joined and flow together toward a goal.

It was this reflection that caused Robinson to become profoundly interested in the marital rites of the creatures surrounding him. He had always recoiled from observing the goats and vultures—in general, all mammals and birds—whose couplings seemed to him a repulsive caricature of human love. But the insects were well worthy of study. He knew that there were varieties which, foraging for nectar, picked up the pollen of the male flower and unconsciously conveyed it to the pistil of the female. The perfection of the process, as he watched it through a magnifying glass in the case of a particular flower known in England as "Dutchman's-pipe," caused him to marvel. No sooner had a bee penetrated the slender corolla of the beautiful blossom than a reflex action made it close. The bee was thus held captive in the most exquisitely feminine of prisons. In struggling to escape, it smothered its hairy legs with pollen, and then, being released by a second reflex, flew off to be imprisoned again elsewhere, the faithful and unknowing servitor of flowery loves.

This process of insemination at a distance, devised by the cruelly separated plants, seemed to Robinson both moving and supremely elegant, and he even dreamed of some fantastic variety of bird which, after charging itself with the seed of the Governor of Speranza, would fly to York to fecundate his deserted wife. But he reflected that being so long without news of him, she must now consider herself a widow, if indeed she had not abandoned widowhood to marry again.

His meditations took another course. He became interested in the proceedings of a male hymenoptera which visited only one variety of orchid, and not, it seemed, for the purpose of foraging. Robinson spent long hours with his glass trying to determine what the creature was doing. He noted first that the flower was an exact reproduction of the abdomen of the female insect, to the point of offering a sort of vagina which probably exuded a specific aphrodisiac scent calculated to attract and seduce the male. The insect did not pilfer the flower for its nectar; rather it *teased* it, and then made love to it according to its own methods of propagation. In doing so its posture was such that the pollen contained in two sacs was deposited on its forehead, where it adhered to two sticky scales; and thus adorned with vegetable scales, the deceived lover flew from male to female flower, serving the orchid species while believing it furthered its own affairs. This wonderful mingling of subterfuge and ingenuity was enough to make one doubt the sobriety of the Creator. Had the natural world been contrived by an infinitely wise and majestic God, or by a baroque Demiurge driven to the wildest whimsicalities by his love of the bizarre? Repressing these doubts, Robinson reflected that there might be trees on the island which, like the orchids with the hymenoptera, might be disposed to make use of himself for the transference of their pollen. And the branches of the trees were transformed in his mind into voluptuous and scented women whose rounded bodies were waiting to receive him. . . .

Searching the island from end to end, he finally discovered a quillaia, or quillai tree, which had been blown over by the wind but not wholly uprooted. The trunk, which lay on the ground, ended in a fork of two main branches rising a little into the air. The bark was smooth and warm, even downy at the point of the fork, where there was a small aperture lined with silky moss.

Robinson hesitated for some days on the threshold of what he later called his "vegetable way." He hung about the quillai with sidelong glances, discovering in the two branches thrusting out of the grass a resemblance to huge, black, parted thighs. Finally he lay naked on the tree, clasping the trunk with his arms while his erect penis thrust its way into that mossy crevice. A happy torpor engulfed him. He lay dreaming with half-closed eyes of banks of creamy-petaled flowers shedding rich and heady perfumes from their bowed corollas. With damp lips parted they seemed to await the gift to be conferred on them by a heaven filled with the lazy drone of insects. Was he the last member of the human race to be summoned to return to the vegetative sources of life? The blossom is the sex of the plant. Innocently the plant offers its sex to all as its most rare and beautiful possession. Robinson lay dreaming of a new human species which would proudly wear its male and female attributes on its head—huge, luminous, scented. . . .

His liaison with Quillai lasted several happy months. Then the rains came. Outwardly nothing was changed, but one day as he lay spread on his strange cross of love a searing pain in his gland brought him sharply to his feet. A big, red-spotted spider ran along the trunk of the tree and vanished into the grass. It was some hours before the pain abated, and his afflicted member looked like a tangerine.

Robinson had suffered many misadventures during his years of solitude amid the flora and fauna of a world enfevered by the tropical sun. But the moral significance of this episode was unavoidable. Although it had been caused by the sting of a spider, could his malady be regarded as anything other than a venereal disease, the "French sickness" against which his masters had so constantly warned him in his student days? He saw in this a sign that the "vegetable way" might be no more than a dangerous blind alley.

CHAPTER SIX

Robinson raised the stem of the sluice gate three holes and secured it with a peg in the fourth. A tremor passed over the glassy surface of the fresh-water reservoir and a green whirlpool took shape, like the corolla of a flower, spinning faster and faster around its stem. A dead leaf drifting at the edge of the pool hung tentatively for an instant and was then sucked in. Robinson turned and stood with his back to the sluice gate, watching the carpet of muddy water as it crept over the flat patch of earth in a bubbling of dry grass, twigs, and patches of foam. When it had reached the far wall of the paddy, thirty yards away, the flow ceased and the level began to rise. An odor of richness and decay rose in the air. Robinson had selected that patch of alluvial land with its clay subsoil for the sowing of half his long-hoarded store of ten gallons of rice. The water would be maintained at the proper level until the plants flowered and he would then allow it to sink and if necessary drain away completely while the ears ripened.

The gurgle of sluggishly moving water soaking into the earth, and the smell of stagnation, sharply evoked the memory of the mire. Robinson was torn between his triumph and a sense of sickening weakness. The rice paddy represented the taming of the mire, a decisive victory over everything most primitive and disturbing in Speranza. But it was a victory at a high price, and he would not easily forget the extreme effort it had cost him, the diversion of the stream to fill his artificial reservoir with its clean-cut clay walls, the digging of ditches, the building of the wooden barriers and the sluices lined at the bottom with stones to prevent erosion: all this so that in ten months' time—and after the husking, which in itself would take some weeks— a consignment of rice might be added to the wheat and barley with which his granary was already overflowing. Once again solitude condemned his toil in advance. He was suddenly and heart-rendingly conscious of the vanity of all his work. What purpose did they serve, the tillage, the stock-breeding, the hoarding, the Charter, the Penal Code? Who was to be nourished by them, who protected? Everything he did, every task he undertook, was an appeal to some other person that met with no response.

Jumping the irrigation ditch, he strode away, his eyes blurring over in despair. Why not destroy it all, burn the crops, blow up the buildings, open the enclosures and lash the goats so that they scattered in all directions? He imagined an earthquake shattering Speranza to fragments, and the waters closing over that purulent crust of which he was the unhappy consciousness. He was convulsed with sobbing. Plunging through a copse of sandalwood and gum trees, he reached a plateau of sandy grass and flung himself on the ground, seeing nothing but the lightning flashes in the red darkness behind his lids, hearing nothing but the tribulation that beat like a tempest in his veins.

It was not the first time, certainly, that the completion of a large task had left him empty and exhausted, a ready prey to despair; but he was beginning to feel more and more often that the cultivation of the island was a meaningless enterprise. It was at these moments that a new man seemed to be coming to life within him, wholly alien to the practical administrator. The two men did not yet coexist in him; they came by turns, each excluding the other; and the danger was that the first of the two, the administrator, might vanish for good before the new man was fully grown.

Failing an upheaval, there were tears, whose salt flow eventually dissolved the knot of exasperation and depression that threatened to choke him. A gleam of sanity returned. He realized that in the ordering of the island lay his only salvation, until such time as another kind of life—impossible to imagine, but already struggling into being within him— was ready to take the place of the very civilized behavior he had clung to since the shipwreck. He must continue his labors, while observing in himself the symptoms of his own metamorphosis.

He fell asleep. When he opened his eyes and rolled over on his back, he found that the sun was setting. The breeze stirring the grass seemed a sigh of compassion. Three pine trees were brushing their branches together, almost fraternally, as though in a gesture of consolation. Robinson felt his lightened spirit soar upward toward a great argosy of cloud which was sailing majestically across the sky. A wave of tenderness passed through him. And now it was that he felt the certainty of change—in the weight of the atmosphere, perhaps, or in the very breath of the world. He was in that *other island,* the one he had once glimpsed but never seen again. He felt as never before that he was lying on Speranza as though on a living being, that the island's body was beneath him. Never before had he felt this with so much intensity, even when he walked barefoot along the shore that was teeming with so much life. The almost carnal pressure of the island against his flesh warmed and excited him. She was naked, this earth that enveloped him, and he stripped off his own clothes. Lying with arms outstretched, his loins in turmoil, he embraced that great body scorched all day by the sun, which now exuded a musky sweat in the cooler air of the evening. He buried his face in the grass roots, breathing open-mouthed a long, hot breath. And the earth responded, filling his nostrils with the heavy scent of dead grass and the ripening of seed, and of sap rising in new shoots. How closely and how wisely were life and death intermingled at this elemental level! His sex burrowed like a plowshare into the earth, and overflowed in immense compassion for all created things. A strange wedlock, consummated in the vast solitude of the Pacific! He lay exhausted, the man who had married the earth, and it seemed to him, clinging timorously like a small frog to the skin of the terrestrial globe, that he was swinging vertiginously with her through infinite space. . . . Finally, a little giddy, he got to his feet and stood for a moment in the breeze, receiving the warm obeisance of the three pine trees, whose silent applause was distantly echoed by the waving green crests of the forest fringing the horizon.

He was standing in a gently rolling meadow broken by folds and slopes dressed in a covering of round-stemmed, pink-tinted grass, like a coat of hair. "It's a coomb," he murmured to himself. "A pink coomb." And this word vaguely suggested another to his mind, somehow related to it, which seemed to endow it with a new and far richer significance; but he could not recall the other word. He stood seeking to retrieve it from the well of forgetfulness in which it had long been buried. Coomb . . . coomb . . . comb. A comb. He had a sudden vision of a comb in a woman's hair, and then of hair flowing down the naked back of a woman running a little to fat but still majestic in her bearing. There was a swell of muscle around her shoulder blades and below this the smooth expanse of flesh narrowed and was then thrust outward in a firm and gently rounded hillock divided by a central fold and covered by a hint of golden down. The woman turned smiling to face him and he saw the soft curve of her belly, the triangle at the meeting of her thighs, the offer of her loins. Her loins. The word came suddenly to Robinson, and it was the word he had been seeking. The loins . . . His hand resting on that tufted mound within which were stored the cravings of spasm and release, the heat, the ardor and the essence, the well of humankind . . . The loins . . . He turned and went back to the Residence with the word singing in his ears.

Journal

That strange amazement with which we open our eyes in the morning! Nothing better testifies to the fact that sleep is an experience in its own right, and as it were a rehearsal of death. Of all the things that can happen to the sleeper, awakening is certainly the one he least expects, and the one for which he is least prepared. No nightmare can so greatly dismay him as that sudden return to light, another light. There can be no doubt that for the sleeper the act of sleeping is final. The soul has taken flight from the body without a backward look or thought of return. It has forgotten everything, cast everything aside, when suddenly and harshly it is compelled to resume the discarded garment of flesh, its habits and its life. . . .

So presently I shall lie down and let myself slip into the darkness forever. A strange alienation. The sleeper is a mind unhinged that thinks itself dead.

The problem of existence. If someone had told me a few years ago that the absence of my fellows would cause me to doubt my own existence I would have laughed, just as I did when "universal consent" was offered as a proof of the existence of God. "The majority of men at all times and in all places have believed in the existence of God. Therefore God exists." How absurd! The most absurd of all the proofs of the existence of God, miserably insufficient compared with that marvel of force and subtlety, the ontological argument.

But now I know otherwise. I know that universal consent is the only proof—and not only of the existence of God.

To exist—what do the words mean? It means to be out-side—sistere ex. That which is outside exists. That which is within does not. My thoughts, images, and dreams do not exist. If Speranza is no more than a sensation, or bundle of sensations, then she does not exist. And I myself exist only insofar as I escape from myself to join with others.

What complicates the position is that the thing which does not exist does its utmost to persuade us of the contrary. There is a great and universal urge toward existence among the non-existent. Something like a centrifugal force seeks to spread outward everything that moves within me, images, dreams, projects, fantasies, desires, obsessions. That which does not ex-sist in-sists. It insists upon existing. All the small world contained within me is knocking at the door of the great, the real world. And it is others, those who are outside, who hold the key. In the past, when I tossed in my sleep, my wife would shake me by the shoulders to wake me and dispel the insistence *of the nightmare. But now . . . But why do I keep returning to this subject?*

All those who knew me, all without exception, believe me dead. My own belief in my existence is opposed to that unanimous belief. No matter what I do, I cannot prevent that picture of Robinson's dead body from existing in all their minds. This alone, though certainly it does not kill me, suffices to remove me to the uttermost confines of life, to a place hung between Heaven and Hell—in a word, to Limbo. Speranza, or the Limbo of the Pacific . . .

This state of half-death at least helps me to understand the deep, positive, and seemingly ineluctable relationship between sex and death. Being closer to death than any other man, I am by the same token closer to the very springs of sexuality.

Sex and death . . . Their close association was first made clear to me in the dissertations of Samuel Gloaming, an elderly York eccentric, a herbalist and taxidermist, whom I visited now and then of an evening in his shop filled with stuffed animals and dried herbs. He had devoted a lifetime's thought to the mysteries of creation, and he said that life was fragmented into an infinite number of entities differing as widely as possible each from the other, so that it might have a no less infinite chance of surviving the vicissitudes of its environment. Were the earth to be frozen to a block of ice, or burned by the sun to a desert of stone, most of the creatures on its surface would perish, but thanks to their variety a few would still remain, capable of adapting themselves to the changed conditions. It was this multiplicity of creatures which in his view made reproduction necessary, that is to say, the transference of life from the old to the new; and he insisted that this was a sacrifice of the individual to the species, since in the act of procreation the individual loses something of his substance. Thus sexuality is the living presence, ominous and mortal, of the species in the essence of the individual. To procreate is to bring forth a new generation which innocently but inexorably will thrust its predecessor toward extinction. No sooner do the parents cease to be indispensable than they begin to become burdensome. The child casts aside his parents as naturally as he took from them all that he needed for his growth. The instinct which brings the sexes together is then an instinct of death. But Nature has thought it prudent to disguise her stratagem, transparent though it is, and what appears to be the self-indulgence of lovers is in reality a course of mad self-abnegation.

I had been pondering these matters when I had occasion to visit a part of northern Ireland which was grievously afflicted by famine. The survivors strayed like ghostly skeletons along the village streets, and the bodies of the dead were burned on pyres to guard against the risk of plague, more deadly than the famine itself. Most of the corpses were male, so true is it that women are capable of greater endurance than men, and they told a strange story: emaciated though they were, drained of substance like leathern dolls of string and bone, the sexual organ, and this alone, was monstrously and ironically enlarged, more rigid and distended, in a word more triumphant, than probably it had ever been in life. This apotheosis in death of the genitals shed an added light on Samuel Gloaming's words, evoking in my mind a dialogue between the individual, the affirma-

tion of life, and sex, the affirmation of death. By the light
of day man in his right mind represses what is undesirable,
he diminishes and disdains it; but under the influence of
darkness, warmth, and languor the enemy revives, unsheathes
his sword, and diminishes the man, makes of him a lover,
plunges him into a brief ecstasy, then closes his eyes—and
the lover, couched on earth, lost in the rapture of forgetfulness and renunciation of self, sinks into that little death
which is sleep.

Couched on earth . . . Those words, flowing naturally
from my pen, are perhaps the key. Earth irresistibly draws
the enclasped lovers with joined lips, cradling them after their
embrace in the happy slumber of sensual delight. But earth
also harbors the dead, sucks their blood and devours their
flesh, that these orphans be restored to the cosmos from
which for the length of a lifetime they were parted. Love
and death, two aspects of the defeat of the individual, turn
with a common impulse to the earth. Both are of their nature earthly.

The more sagacious among men are conscious of this relationship, though they may not clearly perceive it. To me
in my unique situation it is crystal-clear, indeed I am forced
in my entire being to live it. Lacking a woman, I am reduced
to immediate loves. Deprived of that fruitful byway which
a woman's body affords, I must turn directly to the earth
which will be my last resting place. What happened in the
pink coomb? I dug my grave with my sex and died the
transient death that we call pleasure. And I note that in
doing so I have accomplished a further stage in the metamorphosis I am undergoing. For it has taken me years to reach
this point. When I was cast ashore I was still a creature

molded by society. The mechanism which directs sex from its natural tendency toward the earth to the living sheath of a woman was still active in my loins. I wanted a woman or nothing. But solitude has simplified me. Since that byway is closed, the mechanism has become obsolete, and in the pink coomb my sexuality returned to its original source, the earth. Moreover, this further stage in my dehumanization occurred at the very moment when my alter ego had completed, in the building of the rice paddy, the most ambitious human project I have embarked on since I came to rule over Speranza.

How fascinating this tale would be if I were not its sole protagonist, and if it were not written with my blood and tears!

"Thou shalt also be a crown of glory in the hand of the Lord, and a royal diadem in the hand of thy God.

"Thou shalt no more be termed Forsaken; neither shall thy land any more be termed Desolate; but thou shalt be called Hephzibah and thy land Beulah: for the Lord delighteth in thee, and thy land shall be married."

Standing at his lectern in the doorway of the Residence, with the open Bible before him, Robinson recalled that in the distant past he had named the island Desolation. But this morning shone with a nuptial splendor, and Speranza lay prostrate at his feet in the tenderness of the rising sun. A herd of goats were coming down a hillside, and the kids, delighting in the slope and the press of life within them, were leaping and skipping like bouncing balls. To the west the golden sweep of a field of ripe wheat swayed under the caress of a warm breeze. A cluster of palms half-hid the silvery glitter of a rice paddy dotted with young shoots. The great cedar by the mouth of the cave sang with an organ note. Robinson turned the pages of the Book of Books, and what he now read was no other than the love song of Speranza and her spouse.

"*Behold, thou art fair, my love; behold, thou art fair; thou hast doves' eyes within thy locks: thy hair is as a flock of goats, that appear from mount Gilead.*

"*Thy teeth are like a flock of sheep that are even shorn, which came up from the washing; whereof every one bear twins, and none is barren among them.*

"*Thy lips are like a thread of scarlet, and thy speech is comely: thy temples are like a piece of a pomegranate within thy locks.*

"*Thy neck is like the tower of David builded for an armoury, whereon there hang a thousand bucklers, all shields of mighty men.*

"*Thy two breasts are like two young roes that are twins, which feed among the lilies.*"

And Speranza replied:

"*My beloved is gone down into his garden, to the beds of spices, to feed in the gardens, and to gather lilies.*

"*I am my beloved's, and my beloved is mine: he feedeth among the lilies.*

"*Thou art beautiful, O my love, as Tir-zah, comely as Jerusalem, terrible as an army with banners.*

"*I went down into the garden of nuts to see the fruits*

*of the valley, and to see whether the vine flourished, and
the pomegranates budded.*

*"Or ever I was aware, my soul made me like the chariots
of Ammin-a-dib."*

And finally she said, as though in answer to his meditation
on sex and death:

*"Set me as a seal upon thine heart, as a seal upon thine
arm: for love is as strong as death . . ."*

Thus Speranza was henceforth endowed with words.
There was no longer only the rustle of the wind in the
trees, or the surge of the unresting sea, or the peaceful
crackle of the night fire with its twin reflection in the eyes
of Tenn. The Bible, with its imagery identifying the woman
with the earth, the wife with the garden, graced their love
with the most ancient of epithalamia. Before long Robinson
had all the burning lines by heart, and as he walked through
the wood of gum trees and sandalwood on his way to the
pink coomb, he spoke the words of the husband and was
silent while he listened to the wife's reply. Then he was
ready to fling himself into a fold of sand and, setting Speranza
like a seal upon his heart, appease in her his anguish and his
desire.

Nearly a year passed before he perceived that his love was
bringing about a change in the vegetation of the pink coomb.
He had taken no notice at first of the disappearance of
grasses and small seedlings from the places where his own
seed was sown. But his attention was caught by the growth
of a new plant that he had seen nowhere else on the island.

The plant had large, lace-edged leaves which grew in clusters at the level of the earth on a very short stalk. It bore white, sharp-scented blossoms with pointed petals and brown, ample berries which largely overflowed their calyxes.

Robinson observed them with curiosity, but thought no more about them until the day when it became unmistakably apparent that they appeared within a few weeks at the precise place where he had sown his seed. Thereafter he ceaselessly pondered the mystery. He sowed his seed in the earth near the cave, but to no avail. It seemed that these plants could grow nowhere but in the pink coomb. Their strangeness restrained him from plucking them and dissecting and tasting them, as he might otherwise have done. He sought to dismiss the riddle from his mind, since it seemed to have no answer; but suddenly light was shed by a verse from the Song of Songs which he had repeated a thousand times without attaching any special importance to it. *"The mandrakes give a smell,"* sang the young wife, *"and at our gates are all manner of pleasant fruits, new and old, which I have laid up for thee, O my beloved."* Could it be that Speranza was keeping that biblical promise? He had heard of the miracle of the plants, such as nightshade, which grow at the foot of gibbets, where the hanged have let fall their last drops of semen, and which are held to be the fruit of the crossing of man with earth. On the day when this thought occurred to him, he ran to the pink coomb and, kneeling beside one of the plants, very gently lifted it out of the ground, digging round the root with his hands. It was true! His love-making with Speranza was not sterile. The white, fleshy, curiously forked root bore an undeniable resemblance of the body of a woman-child. Trembling with delight and tenderness, he put the mandrake back, and pressed the earth around it as one puts a child to bed. Then he walked away on tiptoe, taking great care not to crush any of the other plants.

Thenceforward, blessed by the Bible, a stronger and more intimate bond united him with Speranza. He had humanized her whom he could henceforth call his wife in a manner that went incomparably deeper than all the enterprises of the Governor. That this closer union represented a further step in the shedding of his human self was something of which he was certainly aware, but he did not measure its extent until he perceived, when he awoke one morning, that his beard, growing in the night, had begun to take root in the earth.

CHAPTER SEVEN

"Do not waste time, it is the stuff of life."

Seated in a sort of sling made of lianas, Robinson thrust himself away from the rock face on which he had painted these words. The letters stood out bold and white against the granite surface. The site was particularly favorable. Every word seemed to be hurtling outward in silence toward the haze of the horizon fringing the vast glitter of the sea. During recent months the chance play of his memory had brought back tags from Benjamin Franklin's *Poor Richard's Almanack*, which his father held to be the quintessence of moral wisdom, and had made him learn by heart. Stakes of wood planted in the sand dunes proclaimed that "Poverty robs a man of all virtue: it is hard for an empty sack to stand upright"; and encrusted in the wall of the cave was a sort of mosaic, which read: "If lying is the second vice, the first is indebtedness: for lies ride on the back of debts." But the greatest of these aphorisms was destined to blaze in letters of fire on the beach, on some night when Robinson felt impelled to defy the darkness with a flaming assertion of truth. Pine cones wrapped in tow, ready to be lit, were arranged on stones in a pattern which proclaimed: "If knaves knew all the advantages of virtue, they would turn virtuous out of knavery."

The island was covered with fields of cereal and vegetables, the rice paddy would soon yield its first harvest, the goat pens were filled, and the cave overflowed with a store of foodstuffs sufficient to maintain the population of a village for several years. Yet Robinson felt this magnificent achievement inexorably draining away. The cultivated island was losing its soul as it gave way to the *other island*, so that it resembled a great machine spinning in a vacuum. This had first caused him to reflect that the cultivated isle, fostered with such prudent economy, might yield a system of morals of which the principles were laid down in Master Franklin's writings; and so he had set about inscribing these on stone and earth and wood, in the very flesh of Speranza, to endow her great body with a soul that suited it.

Carrying his goat-hair brush in one hand, and in the other the pot of fine-ground chalk liquefied with holly sap, Robinson set out to find a suitable site for yet another aphorism, seemingly materialistic, but affirming a certain mastery over time—"He who kills a sow destroys her progeny unto the thousandth generation; he who squanders a crown piece destroys a mountain of sovereigns."

A herd of goats fled in disorder at his approach. It would be amusing, he reflected, to paint the sentence on 113 goats, one letter to each goat, and let chance determine when, in the course of their endless permutations, they would arrange themselves in the right order and reveal the message. He was toying with this notion, and trying to reckon the mathematical odds, when suddenly he let his brush and paint-pot fall, and stood frozen with fear. A column of white smoke was rising into the clear sky. It came, as on the previous occasion, from the Bay of Salvation, and it had the same thick, milky quality. But this time, the messages painted on the rock face and arranged in the dunes and on the beach would warn the intruders of an alien presence, and they might come in search of him. Followed by Tenn, Robinson ran for the fortress, praying that they had not got there before him. An incident occurred during his panicky flight which he scarcely noticed at the time, but later recalled as a fateful omen. One of the tamest of his billy goats, startled by his rapid movement, lowered its head and charged him. Robinson just managed to avoid it, but Tenn was knocked howling into a clump of fern.

They reached the fortress to find it undisturbed; but what Robinson had not foreseen was the effect on his nerves of the possibility of an attack. The place where the Araucanians had landed was less than a mile away. If they were already moving to attack him, they would have the advantage of surprise as well as of numbers. On the other hand, they might be so preoccupied with their murderous ceremonies that they failed to notice indications that the island was inhabited. The uncertainty was intolerable. He had to know. Accordingly he took down a musket, thrust the pistol into his belt, and, still followed by Tenn, who was now limping, plunged into the undergrowth in the direction of the bay. Then he was obliged to hurry back, having forgotten his spyglass.

There were again three outrigger canoes drawn up on the beach, looking from above like children's toys; but there were more men encircling the fire than on the previous occasion, and it seemed to Robinson, studying them through the glass, that they did not belong to the same tribal group. To judge by the heap of quivering flesh over which two executioners were standing, the ritual had already passed its climax. But something now occurred that looked like a departure from the customary procedure. The witch doctress, springing suddenly to her feet from her crouching position, darted toward one of the men in the circle and pointed to him with a skinny arm, her mouth opening in a flood of imprecations which Robinson could not hear. Clearly she was demanding a second sacrifice. There was a stir in the circle of men, and the executioners, machetes in hand, approached this new offender, who was flung to the ground by the men on either side of him. A machete flashed, cutting away the leather apron which was his only garment. The blade rose again, preparing to descend on his naked body, but as it did so the victim leaped to his feet and made a dash for the trees. Through the spyglass he appeared to be simply leaping in the air with the two executioners behind him; but in fact he was running with remarkable speed, straight in Robinson's direction. Although he was no taller than the rest, he was very much more slender, and built on more athletic lines. He was also darker-skinned and somewhat Negroid in feature, in general different from the other men, and it may have been this which had caused him to be singled out for sacrifice.

He drew nearer rapidly, steadily increasing the distance between himself and his pursuers. Had Robinson not been certain that he was well hidden, he might have thought the man had seen him and was coming to him for help. He had to make up his mind. In another minute he would be confronted by all three Indians, who might be reconciled by the sudden appearance of another potential victim. And at this moment Tenn set up a furious barking. The infernal animal! Robinson seized hold of him, and with an arm around his neck, holding his mouth shut with his left hand, he strove awkwardly to level his musket with the other. He was faced now by a moral problem. If he shot down one of the pursuers he might rouse the whole tribe against him. On the other hand, if he shot the sacrificial victim it might be interpreted as a supernatural act, the intervention of an outraged divinity. He had to take one side or the other, being indifferent to both, and prudence counseled that he should support the stronger. He aimed at the breast of the fugitive, who was now very close; but at the moment of firing, Tenn, making a sudden effort to get free, diverted his aim. It was the first of the pursuers who staggered and fell to the ground. The man behind him stopped, bent over the dying body, stared blankly for a moment at the trees, and finally turned and fled wildly back to his companions.

Crouched in a clump of tree fern, a naked and panic-stricken black man pressed his forehead to the ground, while with one hand he groped for the foot of a bearded and armed white man, clad in goatskin and a bonnet of fur, accoutered with the trappings of three thousand years of Western civilization, and sought to place it on his neck.

Robinson and the Araucanian passed the night within the battlements of the fortress, listening intently to the sighs and murmurs of the forest, different at night, but just as loud as they were by day. Every two hours Robinson sent Tenn out to reconnoiter, his duty being to bark if he detected any human presence. But each time he returned without having given the alarm. The Araucanian, who was wearing an old pair of sailor's trousers which Robinson had made him put on less as a protection against the cold than from his own sense of propriety, was mute and apathetic, seemingly oppressed by both the narrowness of his escape and the extraordinary place in which he found himself. He had

not touched the wheat cake Robinson had offered him, but
he chewed constantly some sort of wild berry, making Robinson wonder for a moment where he had found them.
Shortly before daylight he fell asleep on a pile of dead leaves,
curled up, surprisingly, with Tenn, who was also exhausted.
Robinson knew that some Chilean natives were in the habit
of using a domestic animal to warm them in the chill of the
tropic nights, but he was nevertheless surprised at the readiness with which the dog, generally shy and timid, had accepted this procedure.

Perhaps the Indians were waiting until daylight to attack.
Armed with his pistol, both muskets, and all the powder
and ball he could carry, Robinson set out from the fortress
and reached the Bay of Salvation by way of a wide detour
through the sand dunes. The shore was deserted. The three
canoes and their occupants had gone, taking with them the
body of the man he had shot. Nothing remained but the
black circle of the ritual fire, in which the human bones
were scarcely distinguishable from the sticks of charred
wood. In the act of dropping his assortment of weapons
and ammunition on the sand, Robinson found that he had
rid himself of all the accumulated terrors of the night. He
was shaken by a great burst of uncontrollable, nervous laughter, and when at length he recovered his breath he reflected
that it was the first time he had laughed since the wreck
of the *Virginia*. Was this the first result of his having acquired a companion? Had the gift of laughter been restored
to him with the return of human society, on however modest
a scale? He was to return to that question, but at this moment
another thought occurred to him, much more momentous.
The *Escape!* He had always avoided the scene of that
disastrous failure, which had been the prelude to his period

of total collapse. Nevertheless, the *Escape* was still there with her bow pointing to the sea, waiting for arms strong enough to launch her. Perhaps with the newcomer's aid he would be able to complete that long-abandoned venture, and the youth's knowledge of the archipelago would be invaluable.

Returning to the fortress, Robinson found the Araucanian stripped naked and playing with Tenn. This shamelessness irritated him, as did the friendship that seemed to have sprung up between the boy and the dog. After bluntly indicating that he must put his trousers on, Robinson led him to the clearing where he had built the *Escape*.

The broom had grown so high that the squat little craft looked as though it were afloat on a sea of yellow blossoms rippling in the breeze. The mast had fallen, and here and there the deck planking bulged, doubtless under the influence of rain and sun; but otherwise the hull seemed to be intact. Tenn, who had run ahead, bounded around the vessel several times, revealing his presence in the bushes only by the stir of butterflies in his wake. He jumped suddenly onto the deck, and instantly it collapsed beneath him. Robinson saw him vanish with a startled yelp into the bottom of the hull. Drawing nearer, he saw the rest of the deck planking give way each time Tenn attempted to scramble out. The Araucanian seized hold of the edge of the hull, and, raising his closed fist, opened it under Robinson's nose, allowing a handful of reddish powder to be borne away on the wind. He was laughing. Robinson gave the hull a gentle kick and a cloud of dust rose in the air while a hole appeared in the boat's side. The termites had done their work. The *Escape* was little more than a heap of sawdust.

Journal

*So many bitter disappointments during the past three days,
and so many mortifying setbacks to my pride! God has sent
me a companion, but through some obscure whim of Divine
Wisdom, He has elected to choose one from the lowest
stratum of humanity. Not only is the man colored, a coastal
Araucanian, but he is clearly not of pure blood. Everything
about him points to the half-caste, a South American Indian
crossed with Negro. If he had even attained the age of reason
and were capable of appreciating his own insignificance in
face of the civilization I represent! But I should be surprised
if he is more than fifteen years old, bearing in mind the
extreme precocity of these inferior races, and his childish-
ness moves him to impertinent laughter when I seek to instruct him.*

*Moreover, this unforeseen incursion into the long years of
my solitude has shattered my fragile equilibrium. The Escape has again been the occasion of a humiliating moral
collapse. Despite all the years of sowing and reaping, breeding, building, ordering, lawgiving, even the faintest gleam of
hope was enough to set me plunging toward the deadly
trap in which I once almost succumbed. I must take note
of the warning in a spirit of humble acceptance. I have
grieved long enough over the absence of human companionship, for which all my work on the island has been a vain
appeal. That companionship has now been bestowed on me
in its most primitive and rudimentary form, but this will at
least make it easier for me to mold it to my requirements.
My course is clear. I must fit my slave into the system which*

I have perfected over the years. My success in doing so will be manifest on the day when there is no longer any doubt that Speranza and he have jointly benefited from their meeting. I had to find a name for the newcomer. I did not choose to give him a Christian name until he was worthy of that dignity. A savage is not wholly a human being. Nor could I in decency give him an invented name, although this would perhaps have been the sensible solution. I think I have solved the problem with some elegance in giving him the name of the day on which I saved him—Friday. It is the name neither of a person nor of a common object, but somewhat between the two, that of a half-living, half-abstract entity, a name strongly stressing its temporal character, fortuitous and as it were episodic. . . .

Friday rapidly acquired enough English to be able to understand his master's orders. He learned to plow and sow and reap, to thresh and winnow, grind and cook. He milked the goats, made cheese, collected turtles' eggs and soft-boiled them, dug ditches, saw to the fishponds, trapped vermin, calked the canoe, mended his master's garments, and polished his boots. In the evening, clad in a servingman's livery, he waited at the Governor's table. Then he warmed his bed and helped him to undress, before himself retiring to the litter which he placed by the doorway of the Residence and shared with Tenn.

Friday was utterly docile. The truth is that his spirit had died at the moment when the witch doctress pointed her finger at him, and what had fled for safety was a body without a soul, as blind and unwitting as a duck that runs with flapping wings after its head has been cut off. But the body had not run aimlessly. It had run in search of its soul, which was now in the hands of a white man. Since then Friday had belonged body and soul to the white man. All that his master ordered was right, all that he forbade was wrong. It was good to toil night and day for the functioning of an elaborate system that served no purpose; it was bad to eat more than the portion allotted to him by his master. It was good to be a soldier when his master was a general, a choir-boy when his master prayed, a builder's laborer when he built, a farm laborer when he farmed, a herdsman when he herded, a beater when he hunted, a paddler when he traveled by water, a bedside attendant when he was sick, an operator of the fan, and a killer of flies. It was wrong to smoke a pipe, to go naked, or to hide when there was work to be done. Friday's good will was boundless, but on the other hand he was very young, and there were times when youth was too much for him. Then he would laugh. He would burst into an explosion of laughter, confounding the Governor, the sober-minded mentor, the administrator of the island, and putting him out of countenance. Robinson detested those youthful outbursts, which threw his order into confusion and undermined his authority. It was Friday's laughter which first moved Robinson to strike him. Friday was required to repeat after him the religious and moral axioms which he propounded in measured tones. For example—"God is an all-powerful, omniscient master, infinitely good, merciful and just, the Creator of Man and of All Things." And Friday's laugh rang out, irrepressible, lyrical, and blasphemous, to be extinguished like a snuffed candle by a resounding blow on the cheek. This image of a merciful, all-powerful God had seemed to him irresistibly comic in the light of his own brief experience of life. But no matter;

in a voice now trembling with sobs he dutifully repeated his master's words.

And he provided the Governor with one source of particular satisfaction. Thanks to him, Robinson finally put to use the coins he had saved from the wreck. He paid Friday. He paid him a wage of a half sovereign a month. At first he merely "invested" the money for him, allowing it to accumulate at the rate of 5 per cent; but later, considering him to have attained the age of reason, he handed it over to him with the accumulated arrears. Friday could spend the money on extra rations, small objects of use, trifles brought from the *Virginia*, or simply on buying himself a half-day's repose (a whole day was not purchasable), which he spent in the hammock he had made for himself.

For although Sunday was officially a day of rest, it was not a day of culpable idleness. Rising at dawn, Friday swept and garnished the Meeting Hall. Then he woke his master and recited the morning prayer with him; following which they went together to the Meeting Hall, there to join in a ceremony of worship after the Quaker fashion, lasting two hours. Standing at the lectern, the master read passages from the Scriptures, interrupted by long periods of meditation and enlightened with commentaries inspired by the Holy Spirit. Kneeling on the left side of the Hall, the right being reserved for women, Friday listened devoutly to words such as *sin, salvation, hell-fire, damnation, Mammon,* and *apocalypse,* which if they conveyed no precise meaning to his mind, nevertheless had a magical effect, one of obscure, disturbing beauty. And now and then a picture would emerge —for example, of a man swallowed by a whale who escaped unscathed, of a country beset by a plague of frogs so numerous that they were to be found in the beds and even in the loaves of bread, and of a herd of swine which rushed into the sea, being possessed by devils. On these occasions Friday would feel a tickling in his throat and mirth welling up inside him. With a great effort he would concentrate his mind on suitably dismal subjects, for he dared not think what would happen if he burst out laughing during the Sunday meeting.

After luncheon, which was a longer, more elaborate meal than on weekdays, the Governor, carrying a stick he had made for himself which bore some resemblance to a monarch's scepter, and with his head shaded by a huge goatskin parasol carried by Friday, would make a tour of the island, inspecting his fields, rice paddies, orchards, and herds, his completed works and works in progress, bestowing praise and blame on his follower together with instructions regarding next week's schedule. Since the remaining hours of the day, like those preceding them, could not be devoted to any form of lucrative employment, Friday made use of these to tidy and embellish the island. He weeded pathways, planted flowers outside the buildings, and trimmed the trees that graced the residential quarter. By dissolving beeswax in essence of terebinth colored with dyer's oak, Robinson had produced a handsome polish for which in the past he had found little use, since furniture was scarce and wood floors non-existent on the island. It now occurred to him that Friday might use it to polish the flagstones and cobbles forming the surface of the island's main thoroughfare, the pathway running from the cave to the Bay of Salvation, which he had followed on his first day. On reflection, it seemed to him that the pathway's importance as a historical monument justified the immense labor involved, although the polish would be washed away by the first shower of rain and he had at first had some doubts about ordering Friday to undertake it.

Friday had gained his master's approval with several fortunate contrivances of his own. One of Robinson's problems had always been to dispose of his kitchen waste so as not to attract the notice of the vultures and rats. None of the methods he had tried had been wholly satisfactory. The rats dug up anything he buried, the tides flung back whatever he dumped in the sea, and burning meant that the stuff had to be carried some distance if the smoke of the bonfire was not to pervade the living quarters. Friday's method was to make use of a colony of red ants whose termitary was only a stone's throw from the Residence. Seen at a distance, the garbage deposited on the anthill seemed to be endowed with a quivering life of its own, and it was fascinating to watch viscera and skin and gristle disappear until nothing was left but the cleanly stripped bones.

Friday also showed himself to be adept in the use of the bola, a kind of sling consisting of two or three stones on separate cords joined by a central knot, which, properly handled, can be made to fly through the air like a spinning wheel and wrap itself around anything it encounters. At first he used it simply for catching the goats for milking, but it was also useful for bringing down animals for the pot. Eventually he persuaded Robinson that by the use of larger stones it could be made into an effective weapon of offense, capable of immobilizing and even half-strangling an enemy if it caught him in the right place. Haunted by the fear of another Araucanian invasion, Robinson was delighted to add the simple device to his armory, and they spent hours practicing with it on the shore, using a tree stump the size of a man for a target.

Thus, during the first weeks after Friday's arrival, the administration of the island once again became Robinson's main preoccupation, as he fulfilled his roles of Governor, Commander in Chief, and Spiritual Pastor. For a while he even believed that the newcomer would provide a justification for his structure, a weight and stability that would finally do away with the dangers threatening him, just as some ships are not fully seaworthy until ballasted with a certain amount of cargo. He went so far as to consider another possible danger arising out of the state of permanent tension in which the inhabitants of the island lived, and the excess of consumer goods which overflowed their storerooms. He wondered whether he should counteract this by instituting a regular system of holidays at which there would be feasting and drinking. But he suspected that this last idea, not really compatible with the true spirit of the cultivated island, was subconsciously inspired by his longing for the "other island," a longing temporarily in abeyance but secretly growing stronger within him. Perhaps it was this nostalgia that kept him from being wholly content with Friday's docility, and impelled him to drive and test it to its furthest limits.

Journal

He obeys me implicitly in everything, and it is strange that I should still find cause for complaint. But in his very submission there is something too complete, something almost automatic, which chills me—apart from the dumbfounding laughter which at moments he seems unable to control, and which is like the sudden manifestation of a devil within him. A devil. Yes, Friday is possessed. Indeed, he is doubly possessed, for I must acknowledge that, except for those bursts of demonic laughter, it is I who ordain his every thought and deed.

I do not look for much reason in a man of color—of mixed color, I should say, since he is both Indian and Negro. But at the least he might show affection, and except for his absurd and rather shocking fondness for Tenn, I can discover in him no sign at all of human warmth. I am troubled by a regret which it is painful to avow, but which I am bound to set down. I would never venture to say to him "Love me," because I know all too well that for the first time I should not be obeyed. Yet he has no reason not to love me. I saved his life—unintentionally, it is true, but how can he know that? I have taught him everything, and above all to work, which is our greatest wealth. Certainly I beat him from time to time, but he must surely know that this is for his own good. Yet even in this matter his reactions are disconcerting. One day when I was showing him, rather impatiently perhaps, how to peel and split willow shoots before plaiting them, I made a somewhat sweeping gesture with my hand. To my great astonishment he sprang backward, covering his face with his arm. But it would have been senseless in me to strike him at a moment when I was trying to teach him a difficult skill calling for the closest application on his part. Alas, everything leads me to suppose that in his eyes, and at every moment of the day and night, I am just such a madman. Putting myself in his place, I am filled with pity for this defenseless boy, cast upon a desert island at the mercy of a lunatic. But my own state is even worse, for I see myself reflected as a kind of monster in the gaze of my sole companion, as though in a distorting mirror.

Weary of watching him obey my orders mechanically, without showing any interest in the reason for them, I resolved to carry the matter to its logical conclusion. I set him a task which in every prison in the world is held to be the most degrading of harassments—the task of digging a hole and filling it in with the contents of a second; then digging a third, and so on. He labored at this for an entire day, under a leaden sky and in heat like that of a furnace. For Tenn this furious activity was a wonderfully exciting game. Every hole yielded new and intoxicating smells. Whenever Friday paused to mop his forehead with his forearm, Tenn dashed to the latest hole, burrowed into it with his nose, breathing like a grampus, and rapturously did his share of the digging, scattering the earth between his hind legs. Then he galloped around and around, barking and whining, and returned to intoxicate himself again in the trough where the mud or dark humus mingled with the milky sap of cut roots, as death mingles with life when one has attained a certain depth.

To say that Friday gave no sign of resenting this idiotic employment is not enough. I have seldom seen him work with such good will. He did so, indeed, with a kind of enthusiasm which seems to refute the two alternative theories I had applied to him—either that he is utterly dull-witted, or that he believes me to be mad. I have to look elsewhere, and I find myself wondering whether Tenn's impassioned dance around those wounds gratuitously inflicted on the body of Speranza may not provide the clue; and whether, *in seeking merely to humiliate Friday, I have not committed the unpardonable stupidity of revealing to him the secret of the pink coomb.*

One night, Robinson could not sleep. A pool of moonlight shone on the flagstone floor of the Residence. An owl called in the darkness, and he seemed to hear the earth herself moan with unsatisfied love. His mattress of dried grass felt incongruously soft and unreal. He lay for a while thinking of Tenn's mad, erotic dance around that yawning furrow, that body opened up by the violation of Friday's spade. It was a long time since he had visited the coomb. His daughters, the mandrakes, must have grown big by now! He sat up with his feet in the moonlight and smelled the scent of sap rising in his big body, white as a root. He rose silently, stepped over the entwined bodies of Friday and Tenn, and set out for the copse of gum trees and sandalwood.

CHAPTER EIGHT

When he entered the Residence, Friday saw at once that the water clock had stopped. There was still water in the glass jar, but the hole had been plugged, and the level stood at three o'clock in the morning. It caused Friday no astonishment to find Robinson gone. To his mind the stopping of the clock quite naturally implied the absence of the Governor. Accustomed to take things as they came, he did not ask himself where Robinson was, or if he would come back, or even if he was still alive. Nor did he think of going to look for him. He was wholly absorbed in the contemplation of the familiar objects around him, which the stopping of the clock and Robinson's departure presented in an entirely new light. He was now his own master and master of the island. As though in confirmation of the new dignity conferred upon him, Tenn got lazily to his feet and came and stood in front of him, gazing up at him with nut-brown eyes. Poor Tenn was not as young as he had been, and his round, barrel-like body, his overshort legs, his watery eyes and faded shaggy coat all bore witness to the ravages of age at the end of a well-spent dog's life. But he too seemed conscious of the novelty of the situation, and he waited for his friend to decide what they would do.

What to do? There could be no question of continuing

to water the plot of rape and sorrel, a task necessitated by the drought, or of building the lookout post in the topmost branches of the giant cedar, since these things formed part of Robinson's ordered system, now in suspension until his return. Friday's gaze came to rest on a chest under the table, which was carefully closed but not locked, enabling him to inspect its contents. He dragged it out and, tilting it on end, lifted it onto his shoulder. Then he left the Residence, followed by Tenn.

In the northwestern part of the island, where the meadowland merged into the sand dunes, a cluster of weird, vaguely human shapes occupied the cactus garden which Robinson had established there. He had had misgivings about wasting so much time on an unproductive task, but they were plants that needed almost no attention; and he had transplanted only the more interesting specimens, which were scattered all over the island, to this particular spot, where the soil was especially suited to them. He had done so in memory of his father, whose one passion, apart from his wife and children, had been for the tropical plants which he cultivated in a small conservatory. Robinson, as a small boy, had written their Latin names on wooden tablets stuck in the earth of their flowerpots, and these, by a trick of memory, he had subsequently recalled.

The chest hurt Friday's shoulder, and he let it fall to the ground. The lid burst open, and a sumptuous confusion of rich fabrics and jewels spilled out at the feet of the cacti. At last Friday would be able to indulge his fancy with these treasures which enchanted him, although under Robinson's dispensation they had been merely the appurtenances of ceremony and discomfort. It was not his own body that he wished to embellish, since to him all clothing was an encumbrance, but these mysterious plants with their bloated green flesh and arresting gestures, which seemed to him more appropriate than any human form for the display of these dazzling creations.

He first spread the clothes out on the ground to admire them. He found some flat stones, and on these he arranged the gems as though in a jeweler's shopwindow. Then he spent some time going from one cactus to another, noting their shape and testing the firmness of their flesh with his fingers. They were a strange assortment of vegetable mannequins shaped like candelabra, or like humans with squashed heads, twisted limbs, velvety tails, and venomous-fingered hands adorned with prickly stars. Their flesh was sometimes moist and pulpy, sometimes hard and rubbery, sometimes like green, open wounds exuding a smell of rotting flesh. At length Friday picked up a cloak of black watered silk and spread it with a flourish over the broad shoulders of a *Cereus pruinosus*. Then he draped a coquettish flounce over the swollen buttocks of a *Crassula falcata*. A lace handkerchief served as a garland for the spiky phallus of a *Stapelia variegata*, and he put a pair of gauze mittens on the small, downy fingers of a *Crassula lycopodiodes*. A brocade cap fitted admirably on the woolly head of a *Cephalocereus senilis*. Friday busied himself in this fashion for some time, wholly absorbed in his task, draping and rearranging, standing back to judge the effect, and now and then undressing one cactus to clothe another. He put the finishing touches to his work with the jewels, arranging bracelets, necklets, rings, buckles, crosses, and diadems with equal care and discernment. But having completed it, he spent no time in con-

templating the pageant of lords and ladies and extravagant
monsters he had conjured out of the sand. There was nothing more to do there, so he left, with Tenn still at his
heels.

He crossed the sand dunes, enjoying the sounds of his
own footsteps. He paused and turned to the dog, imitating
the sound, growling with his mouth closed. But Tenn was
not amused; he was finding it difficult enough to plow his
way over the soft sand; and at this added noise his hackles
rose. The ground grew firm again as they came to the shore,
which was largely uncovered at low tide. With his head
flung back in the brilliant morning light, Friday strode rejoicing over the great, flawless arena, drunk with his own
youth and freedom in that boundless place where every
movement was possible and nothing could cut off his vision.
He picked up an egg-shaped pebble and balanced it on his
open palm. It was a composite of pink feldspar crystals
mingled with vitreous quartz flecked with mica, crude but
unequivocal, and he liked it better than the jewels he had
left on the cacti. Its curved surface touched his palm at only
one point, making with it a pure and simple geometrical
pattern. A wave ran up the beach, over the shining surface
of wet sand dotted with small jellyfish, and washed around
his ankles. Friday dropped the egg-shaped pebble and picked
up another that was round and flat, a small opalescent disc
splashed with mauve. He tossed it in his hand. If only he
could fly! If he could turn himself into a butterfly! And the
thought of making the stone fly suddenly delighted his Ariel
soul. He sent it skimming over the water, and it bounced
seven times before sinking without a splash. But this was a
game that Tenn knew. He plunged in after it, swimming

with head raised and nose pointing to the horizon, dived, and came back on the crest of a wave, to drop it at Friday's feet.

They walked eastward for a time, and, after passing the dunes, turned toward the south. Friday picked up random objects, starfish, scraps of wood, shells, cuttlebones, tufts of seaweed, and cast them from him, turning them into prey for Tenn, who ran barking after them. Then they came to the rice paddy.

The reservoir was dry, and the level of water in the paddy was steadily falling. It needed to be kept under water for a month if the plants were to reach their full growth, and Robinson's anxiety had increased every time he visited it.

Friday still had the mauve pebble in his hand. He now skimmed it over the paddy, counting the number of its bounces on the oily surface of the water. It bounced nine times, and Tenn had at once leapt off the bank in pursuit of it. His initial impetus carried him a dozen yards, but then he came to a stop. The water was too shallow for him to swim, and he was engulfed in thick mud. He turned and tried to come back to Friday, but after a first effort that wrenched him clear of the mud, he sank back into it, struggling convulsively. It was clear that he would drown if he were not rescued. Friday paused for an instant, gazing at the murky, treacherous water. Then, seeing what must be done, he ran to the outlet sluice and, passing a stick through the top hole in the stem of the gate, began laboriously to haul it up, using the upright as a lever. As the gate slowly rose, creaking in its grooves, the carpet of slime covering the paddy began to shrink and the water drained away. A few minutes later Tenn reached dry land, a solid mass of mud, but safe and sound.

Leaving him to clean himself up, Friday set off light-hearted toward the forest. The thought that the rice crop was ruined did not cross his mind.

To Friday the stopping of the clock and the absence of Robinson were two aspects of a single event, a break in the established order. To Robinson, Friday's disappearance, the dressing of the cacti, and the drying out of the rice paddy all pointed to the inadequacy and perhaps total failure of his attempts to domesticate the Araucanian. It was rare, in any case, for Friday to do anything of his own accord that did not displease Robinson. He could only escape rebuke by meticulously following instructions, or by doing nothing. Robinson had been obliged to recognize that beneath the show of submissiveness, Friday possessed a mind of his own, and that what came out of it was profoundly shocking and subversive of discipline on the island.

He decided at first to ignore Friday's disappearance; but after two days, yielding to a complex feeling of disquiet mingled with curiosity, vague remorse, and sympathy for Tenn, who was evidently distressed by the boy's absence, he went in search of him. During a whole morning he and Tenn combed the part of the forest into which Friday's tracks vanished. Here and there they discovered signs of his passing, and finally Robinson was forced to conclude that Friday was hiding somewhere in that part of the island, living the life of an outlaw and diverting himself with games which baffled Robinson. Wooden masks, a blowpipe, a hammock of lianas in which lay a figure made of raffia, plumed headdresses, snakeskins, the dead bodies of birds—all these were tokens of a secret world to which Robinson possessed no key. But his mystification reached its height some days later when he came to a stream bordered with small trees not unlike willows. These shrubs had all been uprooted and replanted upside down, with their topmost branches in the earth and their roots in the air. But what lent an air of fantasy to the extraordinary sight was the fact that the plants seemed to have adapted themselves to this strange mishandling. Shoots were beginning to appear on the roots, which suggested that the buried branches had turned themselves into roots and the sap was flowing in the opposite direction. Robinson could not tear himself away from his study of the phenomenon. That Friday should have had the idea and carried it out was disturbing enough in itself. But the shrubs had accepted it, Speranza herself had apparently acquiesced in the extravagance! In this case at least, Friday's whimsical imagination had produced a result which, trivial though it was, had positive aspects and was not purely destructive. Robinson was still brooding over it on his way back from the stream when Tenn came to an abrupt stop at a thick clump of magnolia trees entwined with ivy. After pointing with his body rigid, Tenn moved cautiously forward. He stopped again, sniffing at one of the trunks. And suddenly the tree trunk stirred, while Friday's laugh rang out. Using the juice of some plant, he had painted ivy leaves on his naked body, their coils running up his thighs and around his torso, while his head was camouflaged under a helmet of flowers. Thus transformed into a human plant, and squealing with demented laughter, he executed a wild dance around Robinson before dashing off to the seashore to wash him-

self. Robinson, silently watching, saw him vanish, still dancing, into the shade of the mangroves.

The moon that night shone dazzlingly down on the forest
from a cloudless sky. Robinson closed the Residence, and,
leaving Friday and Tenn to look after each other, made
his way into the sylvan corridors pierced here and there by
rays of silver light. Perhaps hypnotized by the brilliance of
this light, the small creatures whose rustlings generally filled
the undergrowth had lapsed into utter silence. As he drew
near the pink coomb, Robinson felt the stress of his daily
preoccupations loosen its hold on him, and he was filled with
marital tenderness.

Friday was causing him more and more concern. Not
merely did he fail to fit harmoniously into the system, but,
an alien presence, he even threatened to destroy it. Such
destructive blunders as his draining of the rice paddy might
be condoned on the grounds of his youth and ignorance;
but, with every appearance of good will, he was proving
himself utterly unreceptive to principles of order and or-
ganization, planning and husbandry. "He creates more work
than he does himself," Robinson reflected sadly, although
with a slight feeling that he was perhaps exaggerating. Moreover, the strange instinct that enabled Friday to come to
terms with and even win the complicity of animals was
distinctly irritating in the case of Tenn, and nothing less
than disastrous in its effect on the lower orders—goats, rab-
bits, even fish. There seemed to be no way of getting it
into his thick, black skull that the livestock was selected,
rounded up, and fed only for its use as nourishment, and
not for the sake of company, or for mock games of hunting
and fishing. To Friday it was unthinkable to kill an animal

except after a chase or a struggle which gave it a chance of survival—a dangerously romantic concept! Nor could he understand that there were harmful species which had to be fought to the death: he had even made pets of a pair of rats, which he encouraged to breed and multiply! Order was a fragile victory, painfully gained over the natural savagery of the island, and the blows dealt it by the Araucanian were doing it great harm. Robinson could not permit himself the luxury of harboring an unruly element that threatened to break down the edifice it had taken him years to build. But what was he to do?

Reaching the edge of the forest, he paused for a moment, spellbound by the beauty and tranquillity of the moonlit scene. The meadowland drifted away into shadow like a silken cloak fluttering here and there in the faint breeze. Beyond it, where the dense cluster of reeds stood up stiffly like the raised lances of an army, he could hear the thin croaking of a tree frog. A white owl brushed past him with its wings and came to rest in a cypress, turning toward him its startled, dreamlike face. A breath of perfume told him that he was approaching the pink coomb, whose soft ridges the moonlight threw into sharp relief. The mandrakes were now so numerous that the whole aspect of the place had changed. Robinson sat with his back against a hummock of sand and reached out a hand to the broad, purple-tinted leaves with their jagged edges, which he had introduced to the island. His fingers encountered the rounded shape of one of their brown fruits, which had a heavy, fetid smell, not easily forgotten. His daughters were there, the blessing of his union with Speranza, spreading their lace-edged petti-coats over the dark grass, and he knew that if he pulled one of them out of the earth he would unveil the white, plump legs of her vegetable form. He lay down in a furrow which was somewhat pebbly, but deep enough to enclose him, and abandoned himself to the sensual torpor, rising from the earth, that penetrated his loins, while⌐he pressed the warm, musky flesh of a mandrake blossom to his lips. He knew every one of those flowers from having counted their blue, violet, white, or purple calyxes. But suddenly he started. The blossom in his hand was *striped!* It was white with dark markings. He shook himself into bewildered wakefulness. This particular plant had not been in flower two days before, when he had visited the coomb by daylight, or he would have been struck by the new variant. In any case, he kept a meticulous chart of his seedings, and he would consult it when he got back to the Residence. But he was positive already that he had never before lain in the place where the striped mandrake was now in bloom.⌐

He stood up. The charm was broken, all the blessing of that radiant night dispelled. A suspicion, still vague, was forming in his mind, which turned at once into rancor against Friday. The secret life, the willow shrubs planted upside down, the strange disguise—even the dressed cacti and Tenn's dance over Speranza's wounds—were not these all clues to the mystery of the new mandrakes?

Journal

I returned to the Residence in a state of extreme agitation. My first impulse was, of course, to awaken the rogue, beat him until he confessed, and then beat him again to punish him for the crimes confessed. But I have learned never to act in anger. Anger impels us to action, but the action is always bad. I forced myself instead to stand erect at the lectern with my heels pressed together and read a passage taken at random from the Bible. It was a hard struggle, with my fury leaping within me like a kid pegged down with a tether that's too short. At length calm returned to me as the majestic and bitter words of the Book of Ecclesiastes resounded from my lips. O Book of Books, how many hours of serenity do I not owe to you! To read the Bible is to be raised to a mountain peak from which I can encompass at a glance the whole island, and the immensity of waters surrounding it. With all pettiness swept away, my soul can spread its wings and soar, knowing only sublime and eternal things. The lofty pessimism of King Solomon was well fitted to appease the anger in my heart. It pleased me to read that there is no new thing under the sun, that all is vexation and vanity of spirit, that there is no remembrance of the wise more than of the fool, that it is vain to build and labor, to sow and reap, since all things turn to dust. It was as though the Sage of Sages were humoring my splenetic mood to prepare me for the one truth that was applicable in my case, which might indeed have lain in waiting through the ages for this moment. And when I came to them, the lines smote me like a corrective blow on the cheek.

"Two are better than one; because they have a good reward for their labour.

"For if they fall, the one will lift up his fellow: but woe to him that is alone when he falleth; for he hath not another to help him up.

"Again, if two lie together, then they have heat: but how can one be warm alone?

*"And if one prevail against him, two shall withstand him;
and a threefold cord is not quickly broken."*

*I read and reread those words and was still repeating them
when I retired to my couch. For the first time I asked myself
if I had not sinned gravely against Charity in seeking by
every means to compel Friday to submit to the laws of the
cultivated island, since in doing so I proclaimed my preference, over my colored brother, for the earth shaped by my
own hands. Truly an ancient dilemma, the source of many a
conflict and countless crimes.*

Robinson forced himself to forget about the striped mandrakes, and was assisted in this by the urgent necessity of
terracing and rebuilding after a series of torrential rains,
which brought him closer to Friday. The months passed in
an alternation of stormy disagreements and tacit reconcilia-
tions. Although at times Robinson was profoundly shocked
by his companion's doings, he concealed his vexation and
later sought to excuse him when he sat down to write his
journal. This happened in the case of the turtle-shell shield.

Friday had been absent that morning for some hours when
Robinson noticed a column of smoke rising above the trees
from the direction of the beach. The lighting of fires on the
island was not expressly forbidden, but the law required that
due notice should be given, specifying the time and place,
so that they might not be attributed to a new landing of the
Araucanians. If Friday had neglected this precaution it could
only be for reasons of his own; in other words, because he
was intent on doing something which would incur his master's displeasure.

Closing his Bible with a sigh, Robinson whistled to Tenn and went down to the beach.

At first he could not understand what Friday was up to. He had rolled a large turtle onto its back on a heap of glowing cinders. The creature was by no means dead. Its legs were frantically waving, and Robinson thought he heard a hoarse, coughing sound which must be its cry of agony. To torture an animal in this fashion was abominable. Friday must be possessed by a devil! Robinson began to understand what he was doing when he saw that the shell was gradually losing its concave shape under the influence of the heat, while Friday was hard at work cutting the ligaments that attached it to the turtle's body. The shell was still not quite flat, more like a slightly curved tray, when the animal succeeded in rolling out of it and getting to its feet. Its back was a pulp, a hideous red and green distension like a bag bulging with blood and pus. With nightmare speed, moving as fast as Tenn, who ran barking behind it, it made for the water and plunged into the waves. "That's a mistake," said Friday calmly. "The crabs will eat it." He was now scouring the inside of the flattened shell with sand. "No arrow will pierce this shield," he explained to Robinson. "Even a heavy bola can't break it."

Journal

It is typical of our English nature to show more mercy toward animals than to men, an attitude of mind which is perhaps open to dispute. The fact remains that nothing has so set me apart from Friday as his unspeakable torture of

*that animal. Yet his is not a simple case and it raises many
questions.*

*I thought at first that he felt affection for my animals.
But his instant and seemingly instinctive understanding with
them—with Tenn, with the goats, even with the rats and
vultures—has nothing in common with my own sentimental
fondness for my fellow creatures. It would seem indeed that
his relationship to animals is itself more animal than human.
He is on their level. He never seeks to improve their lot,
still less to make them love him. He treats them with a
casual indifference, a cruelty, that revolts me but does not
seem at all to diminish their friendliness toward him. The
bond of complicity, it seems, goes deeper than any torment
he may inflict on them. When it dawned upon me that he
would not hesitate, in case of need, to cut Tenn's throat
and eat him, and that the dog's obscure awareness of this
did not in any way affect its preference for him over myself, I felt both anger and jealousy at the animal's stupidity
and blindness to self-interest. But then I realized that we
may only compare like with like, and that Friday's relationship with animals is wholly different from my own. They
accept him as one of themselves. He owes them nothing and
may in innocence exercise over them all the rights conferred
upon him by his superior strength and cunning. I seek to
persuade myself that in so doing he makes manifest the animal in himself.*

Not long after this, Friday became interested in a fledgling
vulture which he rescued after its mother had turned it out
of the nest for reasons of her own. Its ugliness might have

justified the expulsion, had it not been typical of the species. The featherless, misshapen, lurching little creature greeted all comers with a gaping beak at the end of a naked neck, above it two enormous, closed lids, violet-tinted, like boils swollen with matter.

Friday at first thrust scraps of fresh meat into its mouth, and these were gulped down with an eagerness suggesting that it would have swallowed pebbles just as readily. But a day or two later the little creature fell sick. It grew lethargic and spent most of the time sleeping. When Friday felt its crop he found it hard and distended with food, although some hours had elapsed since its last meal. In a word, it showed symptoms of acute and possibly fatal indigestion.

Then Friday put some goat's entrails to cook in the sun, where they lay in a cloud of flies, giving off a stench that turned Robinson's stomach but seemed to revive the vulture's appetite. And when a quantity of small white grubs appeared on the nauseous, half-liquid mess, Friday performed an operation which Robinson was never to forget. Scraping at some of it with a shell, he put it in his mouth, grubs and all, and sat methodically chewing while he gazed absently about him. Then, bending over his foster child's beak, which was held out to him like a blind man's begging bowl, he let the unspeakable white pap dribble into it, while the little creature quivered with delight.

"Living worms are too fresh," he explained to Robinson. "The little bird is ill, so chew-chew. Always chew for little birds."

Robinson fled with his stomach heaving, but Friday's devotion and calm logic greatly impressed him. For the first time he questioned his white man's sensibilities, his queasy fastidiousness, wondering if this were a last rare token of civilization, or only a dead weight that he must be willing to shed before embarking upon a new way of life.

But there were times when the Governor, the General, and the Pastor gained the upper hand in Robinson. His mind dwelt on the ravages caused by Friday in the smooth functioning of the island, the ruined crops, the wasted stores, and scattered herds; the vermin that multiplied and prospered, the tools that were broken or mislaid. All this might have been endurable had it not been for a certain quality of Friday's mind, manifested in the tricks and devices, the diabolical or impish notions he acted upon, spreading around him a confusion which infected Robinson himself. And the sum of his grievances was contained in the striped mandrake, the thought of which haunted him and gave him sleepless nights.

It was in one of his fits of rage that he made himself a whip out of plaited strips of goat hide. He did so with a feeling of secret shame, dismayed by the growth of hatred in his heart. Not merely was Friday playing havoc with Speranza, he was poisoning his master's soul! Indeed, Robinson was beginning to have thoughts which he dared not avow, all centered on the theme of Friday's death, natural, accidental, or contrived.

Things had reached this pass when one morning a fateful presentiment drew his footsteps to the copse of gum trees and sandalwood. A splash of brilliant color flew out of a clump of thuya and rose circling into the air, a gigantic, splendid butterfly with wings of black velvet and gold. The whiplash whistled and cracked, and the living flower flut-

tered in fragments to the earth. This was another thing
Robinson would not have done a few months earlier. . . .
It was true that the fire he felt blazing within him seemed
to him more exalted, purer in its essence, than any simple
human passion. As in all things affecting his relations with
Speranza, there was something cosmic in his fury. He did
not see himself in commonplace terms, as a plain man en-
raged, but as a primitive force issued from the bowels of
the earth to sweep all things away with its scorching breath.
A volcano. A volcano bursting through Speranza's surface
with the deep-buried fury of rock and alluvial soil. Moreover, for some time past, whenever he had opened the Bible,
it was to hear the thundering of Jehovah.

"*Behold, the name of the Lord cometh from far, burning
with his anger, and the burden thereof is heavy: his lips
are full of indignation, and his tongue as a devouring fire:*
"*And his breath, as an overflowing stream, shall reach to
the midst of the neck, to sift the nations with the sieve of
vanity: and there shall be a bridle in the jaws of the people,
causing them to err.*"

In reading those verses aloud, Robinson could not subdue
his own outbursts, which both soothed and inflamed him.
He seemed to see himself standing on the topmost pinnacle
of the island, terrible and sublime.

"*And the Lord shall cause his glorious voice to be heard,
and shall shew the lighting down of his arm, with the indignation of his anger, and with the flame of a devouring
fire, with scattering, and tempest, and hailstones.*"

The whip cracked again, directed at the form of a vulture soaring lazily high above, far beyond Robinson's reach, but in his fog of exaltation he saw it fall to the ground at his feet, broken and quivering, and he burst into savage laughter.

But in the heart of this desert of despair flowed one source of consolation. The pink coomb with its welcoming folds, its lascivious undulations, was still there, cool and healing in the sweetness of its scented skin. Robinson went more quickly. In a few moments he would be able to stretch himself on that feminine earth, lie on his back with his arms crossed, and it would seem to him that he was plunging into an abyss of blue, bearing all Speranza on his back as Atlas did the terrestrial globe. Then, with strength renewed by contact with that primal source, he would turn to press his loins to the huge, warm female body, to furrow it with a plow of flesh.

He paused at the edge of the forest, with the breasts and groins of the coomb spread out before him. The hand's-breadth leaves of the mandrakes, his daughters, seemed to wave in welcome, and a warmth stirred in his loins and sweet moisture filled his mouth. Signaling to Tenn to wait for him under the trees, he hurried as though borne on wings to his wedded couch. There was a marshy patch enclosing a small, still pool with a scattering of pale sand at its edges overgrown with soft grass. This was where he would make love today. He knew that grassy nook already, and the violet-tinted gold of mandrake blossoms already shone there.

At that moment he saw two small, black buttocks half-buried in the leaves and hard at work, rising and falling, swelling and contracting, like a swift-gathering and receding tide. Robinson stood like a sleepwalker, harshly awakened

from a dream of love. He stood thunderstruck, contemplating the infamy taking place beneath his eyes. Speranza sullied, outraged by a Negro! The striped mandrakes would
be appearing here, too, in a few weeks' time! And he had
left his whip at the edge of the forest with Tenn! He kicked
Friday to his feet, stretched him on the grass again with a
blow of his fist, and then fell upon him with all his white
man's weight and strength. No thought now of love-making!
He beat him with clenched fists like a man deaf and blind,
deaf to the cries that issued from the boy's bleeding lips.
A sacred fury possessed him. He was the Flood drowning
human iniquity over the whole surface of the globe, the fire
from Heaven purging Sodom and Gomorrah, the Seven
Plagues chastising Pharaoh for his hardness of heart. But at
length a few words gasped out by Friday penetrated this
blanket of godlike wrath—"Master, don't kill me!" Robinson's grazed fist fell once more, but halfheartedly, and then
was stayed by a painful reflection. It dawned upon him that
he was enacting another, long-familiar scene, a scene of
brother beating brother to death at the side of a ditch, the
first murder in recorded history, the murder of all murders.
Who was he, then? Was he the avenging arm of Jehovah,
or was he marked by the curse of Cain? He got to his feet
and turned and ran to cleanse himself in the source of all
wisdom. . . .

Again he stood at the lectern, heels together and hands
joined, awaiting the guidance of the Holy Spirit. He wanted
to dignify his anger, and give it a purer, loftier tone. Opening the Bible at random, he came upon the Book of Hosea.
The words of the prophet sprang at him, black upon the
white page, as lightning precedes thunder, before they re-

sounded from his lips. And it was to his daughters, the mandrakes, that he was speaking, warning them against their
mother, the adulterous earth:

*"Plead with your mother, plead: for she is not my wife,
neither am I her husband: let her therefore put away her
whoredoms out of her sight, and her adulteries from between her breasts:*

*"Lest I strip her naked, and set her as in the day that she
was born, and make her as a wilderness, and set her like a dry
land, and slay her with thirst."*

The Book of Books had spoken, and it was Speranza who
stood condemned! This was not what Robinson had looked
for. He had wanted to read in letters of fire the condemna-
tion of the unworthy servant, the seducer and violator. He
closed the Book and opened it again at random. Now it was
Jeremiah who spoke, and he spoke of the striped mandrakes
in the image of the strange vine:

*"For of old time I have broken thy yoke, and burst thy
bands; and thou saidst, I will not transgress; when upon
every high hill and under every green tree thou wanderest,
playing the harlot.*

*"Yet I had planted thee a noble vine, wholly a right seed:
how then art thou turned into the degenerate plant of a
strange vine unto me?*

*"For though thou wash thee with nitre, and take thee
much soap, yet thine iniquity is marked before me, saith the
Lord God."*

But if Speranza had seduced Friday, did this mean that the boy was wholly innocent and blameless? With his outraged heart in rebellion against this verdict that condemned Speranza, and her alone, Robinson again closed and opened his Bible. He opened it at the Book of Genesis, and read aloud as follows:

"And it came to pass after these things, that his master's wife cast her eyes upon Joseph; and she said, Lie with me.

"But he refused, and said unto his master's wife, Behold, my master wotteth not what is with me in the house, and he hath committed all that he hath to my hand;

"There is none greater in this house than I; neither hath he kept back any thing from me but thee, because thou art his wife: how then can I do this great wickedness, and sin against God?

"And it came to pass, as she spake to Joseph day by day, that he hearkened not unto her, to lie by her, or to be with her.

"And it came to pass about this time, that Joseph went into the house to do his business; and there was none of the men of the house there within.

"And she caught him by his garment, saying, Lie with me: and he left his garment in her hand, and fled, and got him out.

"And it came to pass, when she saw that he had left his garment in her hand, and was fled forth,

"That she called unto the men of her house, and spake unto them, saying, See, he hath brought in an Hebrew unto us to mock us; he came in unto me to lie with me, and I cried with a loud voice:

"And it came to pass, when he heard that I lifted up my voice and cried, that he left his garment with me, and fled, and got him out.

"And she laid up his garment by her, until his lord came home.

"And she spake unto him according to these words, saying, The Hebrew servant, which thou hast brought unto us, came in unto me to mock me:

"And it came to pass, as I lifted up my voice and cried, that he left his garment with me, and fled out.

"And it came to pass, when his master heard the words of his wife, which she spake unto him, saying, After this manner did thy servant to me; that his wrath was kindled.

"And Joseph's master took him, and put him into the prison, a place where the king's prisoners were bound: and he was there in the prison."

Robinson fell silent in dismay. He was sure that his eyes had not deceived him. He had beyond question surprised Friday in the act of fornication with the earth of Speranza. But he also knew that for a long time past he had needed to interpret external facts, however indisputable, as so many tokens of a deeper truth, still buried and in process of becoming. Friday planting his black seed in the earth of the pink coomb, whether in a spirit of imitation or in sheer impudence, was an incidental happening, as much an anecdote as that tale of Joseph and Potiphar's wife. Robinson was becoming ever more conscious of the gap between the image of the island projected into his mind by his garbled recollections of human society, or his reading of the Bible, and the inhuman, primitive, and uncompromising world whose truth he was timidly seeking. The truth that was in him, which had never deceived him, was warning him in veiled terms that the period of the island-wife—following the period of the island-mother, which itself had followed that of the cultivated island—was now at an end, and that some new development was approaching, utterly strange and unpredictable.

Leaving the lectern, he moved quietly and thoughtfully to stand in the doorway of the Residence. Here he had a movement of recoil, and his anger flared up again, when at his left hand he saw Friday squatted motionless on his heels with his back against the wall of the hut, gazing into space. The boy was capable of remaining like this for hours, in a posture which he himself could not sustain for more than a few minutes without getting severe cramps in his legs. A prey to conflicting emotions, Robinson finally took it upon himself to sit down beside Friday, to commune with him in the deep hush of silent expectation that now enveloped Speranza and its inhabitants.

The sun shone down in all-powerful majesty out of a cloudless sky, casting its golden weight on the sea stretched beneath it in total submission, on the dried and swooning island, on Robinson's buildings, which at that moment were like so many temples consecrated to its splendor. The truth within him murmured to Robinson that perhaps one day the earthly reign of Speranza would be succeeded by a *solar* reign, but the thought was still so vague, so weak and difficult to grasp, that he could not contemplate it for long, and put it aside for a while, to let it ripen in his mind.

Turning his head, he studied Friday's face in profile. Its right side was covered with cuts and bruises, and there was a purple-gaping gash over the high cheekbone. As though he were observing him through a magnifying glass, Robinson considered the prognathous, slightly animal countenance, rendered more than usually stubborn and sulky at that moment by the boy's distress. And it was now that he became aware of something pure and sensitive gleaming amid the unsightly, mishandled flesh. He noted Friday's eye, beneath its long, curved lashes, seeing how the wonderfully smooth and limpid ball was incessantly wiped clean and refreshed by the beating of the lid. He noted the constant widening and shrinking of the pupil, in response to the scarcely perceptible variations of light, as it regulated the message to be transmitted to the retina. Within the transparency of the iris was contained a tiny, intricate pattern like feathers of glass, a cultivated rose, infinitely precious and delicate. It was a beautiful thing, so finely contrived, so perfectly new and shining. How did it come about that this marvel should be part of a creature so coarse, so graceless and uncouth? And if he had only at this moment perceived its beauty, must he not in honesty ask himself whether Friday might not be the sum of other attributes no less admirable, which in his blindness he had failed to see?

Robinson turned the question over in his mind. For the first time he was clearly envisaging the possibility that within the crude and brutish half-caste who so exasperated him another Friday might be concealed—just as he had once suspected, before exploring the cave or discovering the coomb, that another Speranza might be hidden beneath his cultivated island.

But this thought, too, was soon dismissed, and life resumed its arduous and monotonous course.

Life resumed its daily course, but now there was always something in Robinson that awaited a decisive event, something overwhelming, a radically new beginning that would reduce to nothingness all his past undertakings and future plans. The man he had been might protest at this, might continue doggedly to labor, reckoning the amount of next season's harvest, planning new crops of grasses and rare woods, even designing a water mill to be built on one of the streams. . . . But Robinson never went back to the pink coomb.

Friday was troubled by no such problems. He had discovered the tobacco jar, and he smoked Van Deyssel's pipe in secret. His punishment, if he were caught, would certainly be severe, for the tobacco was nearly all gone, and Robinson allowed himself only one pipe every other month. It was an indulgence to which he looked forward long in advance, and he dreaded the day when it would come to an end. He went down one morning to inspect the fishing lines he had laid out at low tide the night before, which should now be uncovered. Friday tucked the tobacco jar under his arm and started off for the cave. He got no pleasure out of smoking in the open air, but if he smoked in any of the buildings the smell would give him away. Robinson could smoke anywhere. For him all that mattered was the spluttering bowl, the earthly container of a small, subterranean sun, as it were a tamed, portable volcano which glowed peaceably under its ashes at the summons of his mouth. In that miniature retort the smoldering tobacco was transmuted into resins and tars whose scented essence agreeably titillated his nostrils. It was the possessed nuptial chamber, held in the hollow of his hand, of the earth and the sun.

For Friday, on the contrary, the delight of smoking lay wholly in the rising eddy of smoke, and the slightest draft robbed it of its charm. He needed to smoke in an absolutely sheltered place, and nowhere suited his airy pleasure better than the motionless air of the cave.

Using sacks and barrels, he had made a sort of chaise longue for himself about a dozen yards from the entrance, and here he reclined, drawing deeply on the horn mouth-piece of the pipe, then allowing a thin stream of smoke to drift upward from his lips, and disappear intact into his nostrils. The smoke thus performed its major function: it pervaded and sensitized his lungs, bringing consciousness and a kind of luminosity to that concealed hollow in his chest which was the most aerial and spiritual part of himself. Finally, he gently expelled the blue cloud. Seen against the light coming from the entrance to the cave, the smoke spread like the tentacles of an octopus, rising in arabesques and slow, spreading coils that grew fainter as they drifted upward. . . . Friday lay dreaming, and he was about to draw again on the pipe when he heard a distant sound of shouting and barking. Robinson had returned sooner than he expected, and he was calling to him in a voice that boded no good. Tenn gave a yelp as the whip cracked. Robinson's voice grew louder, more threatening, and then his figure appeared outlined in the mouth of the cave, striding with clenched fists and the whip whistling above his head. Friday jumped to his feet. What was he to do with the pipe? He flung it with all his strength into the depths of the cave, and then went bravely to meet his chastisement. Robinson must have noticed the removal of the tobacco jar because he was beside himself with fury. He raised the whip . . .

and it was at this moment that the explosion occurred. A great burst of flame swept through the cave. In his last moment of consciousness, Robinson felt himself lifted and hurled backward, while he saw the mass of loose rock above the cave come tumbling down like a child's toy.

CHAPTER NINE

When his eyes opened Robinson found a black face bent over him. Friday was lifting his head with one hand while he tried to get him to drink water from the cupped palm of his other hand. Robinson's mouth closed convulsively, and the water spilled over his beard and chest. Seeing him move, Friday stood up smiling, and a part of his scorched and blackened shirt, and his left trouser leg, fell to the ground. He laughed and wriggled out of the rest of his shredded garments. Then, retrieving a piece of mirror from the debris of their home, he looked at himself in it, pulled a face, and offered it to Robinson, laughing again. Robinson's face was blackened and his red beard was singed, but there was no other sign of damage. He too stood up and stripped off the rags still clinging to him. He walked a few paces. It seemed that he was suffering from nothing more than a few bruises under the thick coating of dust and grime.

The Residence was burning like a torch. The creneleted wall of the fortress had collapsed into the moat. The office building, the Meeting Hall, and the calendar mast, being lighter, had been blown to bits. As Robinson and Friday stood contemplating the devastation, a mass of earth rose into the air some fifty yards away, accompanied by a shattering explosion which again knocked them to the ground. It must have been the charge of powder Robinson had buried outside the walls as a defense against invaders, with a fuse running to the fortress. Not until he was satisfied that all the powder was disposed of did Robinson pluck up enough courage to go and review the disaster.

The goats, terrified by this second explosion, which was much closer to them, had broken down the fence around them and were now bolting in every direction. Within an hour they would be scattered all over the island, and within a week have reverted to their natural state. At the entrance to the cave there was now an avalanche of great boulders shaped like towers, pyramids, prisms, and cylinders, a mountain of rubble dominated by a vertical spire of rock which seemed to offer a beautiful view of the island and the sea. The explosion, in short, had not been merely destructive; where it had been violent, it seemed as if some architectural genius had freely indulged a wild, baroque imagination.

Robinson gazed numbly about him, and began mechanically to pick up the odds and ends that had been blown out of the cave before it collapsed. There were torn clothes, a musket with a twisted barrel, fragments of earthenware, charred sacks, and split baskets. He examined each object in turn before depositing it gently at the foot of the giant cedar. Friday followed his example, but without being very helpful. To preserve and repair was not in his nature, and he was more likely to complete the destruction of the things he handled. Robinson was too stunned to be angry, and he made no protest even when he saw the boy throw away several handfuls of wheat that he found in the bottom of a jar.

It was growing dark, and they had found one object that was still intact, namely the spyglass, when they came upon the body of Tenn stretched under a tree. Friday felt and probed it for a long time. No bones were broken, and it bore no sign of injury, but the old dog was undoubtedly dead. Poor faithful Tenn—perhaps he had simply died of fright! They decided to bury him in the morning. A wind had come up. They went together to wash themselves in the sea, and then made a meal of wild bananas—and Robinson recalled that these were the first things he had eaten on the island. Not knowing where else to sleep, they lay down amid their shattered belongings under the cedar. The sky was clear, but a strong northwesterly breeze was whipping the tops of the trees. The heavy branches of the cedar, however, were scarcely affected by this commotion, and Robinson lay on his back, gazing up at their tranquil, lacy outline, traced like a pattern in Chinese ink against a background of stars.

It seemed, then, that Friday had triumphed at last over the state of affairs he so detested! He had not, of course, deliberately caused the disaster. Robinson well knew that calculations of that sort were quite out of keeping with his character. Friday was not a rational being, performing deliberate, considered acts, but rather a force of nature from which actions proceeded, and their consequences resembled him, the way children resemble their mother. Nothing, it seemed, could blunt his natural spontaneity, and Robinson realized that in this basic matter his influence over the boy was nil. Unwittingly but inexorably Friday had paved the way for, and finally achieved, a cataclysm that heralded the coming of a new era; as for the nature of this new era, clearly it was in Friday's own nature that Robinson must look for it. He was still too much the prisoner of his former self to predict what form it would take. The gulf that separated him from Friday far exceeded, even though it encompassed, the day-to-day antagonisms between the methodical, parsimonious, melancholy-minded Englishman and the laughing, exuberant, uninhibited native of a warmer clime. Friday was instinctively repelled by the sober order which Robinson had imposed on the island, and which had enabled him to survive. It seemed, indeed, that he belonged to an entirely different realm, wholly opposed to his master's order of earth and husbandry, on which he could have only a disruptive effect if anyone tried to imprison him within it.

The explosion had still not quite destroyed the old Robinson: it occurred to him, as he looked at his sleeping companion, that he could very easily kill him—he deserved death a hundred times over!—and then methodically set about the rebuilding of his shattered world. That he did not do so was not only because of his fear of solitude, or his instinctive recoil from such an act of violence. The truth was that the cultivated island had begun to oppress him almost as much as it had Friday. In his heart he had longed for something of this kind to happen. And so, having released him from his earthly bonds, Friday would now show him the way to *something else*, substituting for an existence he had found intolerable a new order which Robinson longed to discover. A new Robinson was sloughing off his old skin, fully prepared to accept the decay of his cultivated island and, at the heels of an unthinking guide, enter upon an unknown road.

He had reached this point in his reflections when he felt a movement beneath his hand as it lay palm-down on the earth. He thought at first that it was some insect, and explored the surface with his finger tips. But it was the earth itself bursting upward. A field mouse, perhaps, or a mole about to emerge from its digging; and Robinson smiled at the thought of the little creature's terror when it found itself trapped in a prison of flesh instead of reaching open air. The earth moved again and something did emerge, but it was something cold and hard that still remained anchored in the soil. A root! It seemed that to crown that day of terror, the very roots were coming to life and thrusting their way out of the ground! In a mood to accept every miracle, Robinson continued to gaze up at the stars through the branches of the tree. He saw a group of stars slide suddenly to the right, vanishing behind a branch to reappear on its other side. There was a brief pause, and then came a hideous sound of creaking and rending. By now Friday had sprung to his feet and was tugging at Robinson's arm. They ran frantically with the ground heaving beneath them, while the crest of the cedar swung slowly through the stars; and with a thunderous sound the great tree crashed down among the other trees, coming to rest among them like a giant fallen into long grass. Its roots, now exposed, held a hillock of earth in their numberless, twisted arms. The crash was followed by an awe-inspiring silence. Its foundations undermined by the explosion, the tutelary genius of Speranza had after all not been able to resist the steady pressure of the night wind sweeping over the island, gustless though it was.

This latest blow to the earthly being of Speranza, following the destruction of the cave, broke the last bond uniting Robinson to the life he had lived before. Henceforward he was a wanderer, foot-loose and timorous, in the sole company of Friday. He would never again let go the hand that had reached down to save him on the night the tree fell.

Friday's freedom, as Robinson discovered in the days that followed, was something more than a mere negation of the order that the explosion had destroyed. Robinson was only too familiar, from his early days on Speranza, with the life of utter purposelessness, at the mercy of every whim and a prey to every frustration, not to realize that at the heart of Friday's way of life there was an underlying wholeness, an implicit principle.

Friday never worked in any real sense of the word. Unconcerned with past or future, he lived wholly in the present. He would lie for days on end in the hammock he had made for himself, slung between two pepper trees, using a blow-pipe to bring down birds which perched in the branches above him, tricked by his immobility; and in the evening he would drop his bag at Robinson's feet with an offhand gesture which might have been that of a faithful retriever or, on the other hand, of a master so sure of his authority that he did not trouble to give orders. But the truth was that their relationship now extended beyond either of those poles. Robinson now observed with a passionate interest Friday's every act, and their effect upon himself, which seemed to lead toward an astonishing metamorphosis.

The first thing to be affected was Robinson's appearance. He gave up shaving his skull and let his hair grow in tangled locks that grew more luxuriant every day. On the other hand, he trimmed his beard, after its singeing by the explosion, and every day he scraped his cheeks with the blade of his clasp knife, painstakingly honed with a piece of the pumice stone that was common on the island. This not only did away with the solemn, patriarchal air, the loftiness of God the Father, which had sustained him in his former dignity; it also made him look ten years younger. A glance in the mirror even told him that, by a perfectly explicable phenomenon of mimicry, there was now a perceptible resemblance between his face and that of his companion. For years he had been both Friday's master and his father. Now in a matter of days he had become his brother, and he was not even sure of being the elder brother. His body had also changed. Having always considered the tropical sun among the worst perils to threaten an Englishman, particularly a fair-skinned, redheaded one, he had taken pains to protect himself against its rays, even to the point of carrying his goatskin parasol. His periods of retreat in the cave, and his later intimacy with the earth, had endowed his skin with the delicate, milky whiteness of underground shoots and tubers. But now, encouraged by Friday, he went naked under the sun. He had done so timidly at first, shrinking and ugly, but gradually he unfolded. His skin turned copper-colored; a new pride swelled his chest and muscles; a warmth flowed through his body from which, it seemed to him, his soul derived a hitherto unsuspected sustenance. In a word, he found that a body which is accepted and rejoiced in—even vaguely desired, with a kind of unconscious narcissism—is not only a better instrument for dealing with the external world, but also a sturdy and loyal companion.

With Friday he engaged in games and exercises which formerly he would have considered beneath him. For example, he was not content until he could walk on his hands as well as Friday. He could stand on them easily enough with his feet against a rock, but as soon as he attempted to move away he fell over, not because his arms lacked the strength to support him, but from insufficient skill and balance. He persevered steadfastly, with a feeling that by acquiring greater versatility in the use of his limbs, he was making progress on the new road he sought to follow. He had visions of his body transformed into one large hand, his head, arms, and legs its five fingers—legs capable of pointing like a forefinger, arms capable of serving as legs, the body capable of resting on any of its limbs like a hand poised on one finger or another.

Among Friday's rare employments was the making of bows and arrows, which he did with a meticulous care that was all the more remarkable because he seldom used them for hunting. After experimenting with various woods for the bows, he discovered a kind of boxwood that he reinforced with strips of goat's-horn to increase its strength and resilience. But he gave particular attention to the arrows, devoting hours to consideration of the weight and thickness of the shafts and the delicate balance between the tip and the "flight." Indeed, from the pains he took with the flights, experimenting with different kinds of feathers and even with leaves, and from his manner of carving the bone tips, it was obvious that he was less concerned with hitting a target than with producing a missile that would travel as far as possible.

When he drew his bow it was with a rapt expression, one of almost painful concentration, as he searched for the correct angle to send his arrow on the most impressive trajectory; and, having released it, he would stand watching its flight with both arms upflung, almost in an attitude of prayer. His face glowed with pleasure so long as it soared upward, but something seemed to snap in him when, losing momentum, it plunged once again downward.

For a long time Robinson was puzzled by this passion for shooting arrows without a target, which Friday pursued to the point of exhaustion. But he came to understand it better on a day when a stiff sea breeze was driving breakers up the beach. Friday was experimenting with a new design of arrow with a particularly long and elaborate flight made of albatross quills. He shot one in the direction of the woods at an angle of forty-five degrees. The arrow rose to a height of some 150 feet; but then, instead of diving back to earth, it hesitated, leveled out, and glided over the treetops out of sight. Friday turned with a glowing face to Robinson.

"It'll fall among the trees," Robinson said. "You'll never find it again."

"No, I won't find it again," said Friday. "Because that one will never fall."

Being restored to their natural state, the goats ceased to live in the state of anarchy that man's domestication imposes on them. They broke up into hierarchical flocks, led by the strongest and wisest males. When danger threatened they clustered tightly together, generally on a high place, and those on the outside confronted the aggressor with lowered horns. Friday amused himself by challenging any male goat he could catch. He would seize them by the horns and throw them, and if he had to chase one he would celebrate his victory by tying a garland of creepers around its neck.

But one day he was himself overthrown by a particularly large and fierce male with huge, knotted horns starting like black flames out of its head. It knocked him backward down a rocky slope, and he had to spend three days in his hammock recovering. During this time he talked of nothing but his return match with the animal, whom he christened Andoar, and for whom he seemed to have developed a true feeling of admiration, mingled with affection. Andoar could be detected at two arrow-flights' distance by his terrible smell; he never ran away when approached; he generally stayed apart from the herd; above all, he had made no attempt to savage Friday after knocking him down, as any other male goat would have done. While he thus sang Andoar's praises, Friday was busy making him a special halter, stronger and more brightly colored than the garlands he had made for the other males. When he again set out for Andoar's rocky domain, Robinson protested mildly, but without hoping to detain him. The stench which clung to Friday after these encounters was in itself a reason for protesting; but in any case they were dangerous, as his recent misadventure had shown. Friday took no notice. He was as lavish in the expenditure of strength and courage in any sport that pleased him as he was feckless and indolent in everyday matters. He had found in Andoar a worthy adversary, and he cheerfully accepted the risk of further injury, even death.

He had no difficulty in finding him. The great male was standing like a rock amid a herd of females and kids which scattered at Friday's approach. They were left alone in a natural arena, bounded at its far end by a slope of rubble overgrown with cactus, and to the west by a precipice one hundred feet deep. Friday untied the halter, which he had twisted around his wrist, and waved it like a gauntlet at Andoar. The goat abruptly stopped grazing and looked up with a stalk of grass hanging from its lips. Then it seemed to grin and reared up on its hand legs; in this position it took several steps toward Friday, waving its forefeet and nodding its immense horns as though acknowledging a throng of spectators. This astonishing performance turned Friday rigid with amazement. When it was within a few yards of him the goat dropped its forefeet to the ground and suddenly charged like a battering-ram—or a great arrow feathered with fur—its head lowered and its horns aimed at Friday's chest. Friday flung himself sideways a fraction of a

second too late. A musky smell filled his nostrils just as a
violent blow on his right shoulder caused him to spin around.
He fell heavily and lay motionless, knowing that if he got
up too soon he would be in no condition to dodge another
charge. He lay on his back gazing with half-closed eyes at
a patch of blue sky framed by stems of dried grass; and
presently he saw a face looking down at him like that of a
Jewish patriarch, with green eyes sunk in shaggy hollows, a
curly beard, a dark muzzle with lips drawn back in a faun-
like grin. With one feeble movement a searing pain shot
through Friday's shoulder, and he fainted. When he again
opened his eyes the sun was blazing into them and its heat
was intolerable. Raising himself on his left arm, he struggled
halfway to his feet, staring dizzily at the rocky slope which
reflected the sun's rays in every direction. Andoar was nowhere to be seen. Friday stood up shakily, and was about
to leave when he heard the sound of hoofs on the stones
behind him. The sound was so close that he did not attempt
to turn around but flung himself to the left, falling on his
sound arm. The blow caught him on the left hip as he fell,
causing him to lurch forward with his arms flung wide. The
goat, its charge broken, came to an abrupt stop beside him,
and Friday swayed, lost his balance, and collapsed limply
like a puppet onto its back. In agony from the pain in his
shoulder, he clung there, gripping the base of the knotted
horns, while he wound his legs around the beast's flanks and
dug his toes into its belly. Andoar executed a series of astonishing leaps in his efforts to rid himself of this burden of
naked flesh. Despite its weight he galloped several times
around the arena without losing his foothold amid the rocks.
Had he fallen, or deliberately rolled over, he would not have
been able to get up again. Friday by now was in so much

pain that he was afraid of losing consciousness again. He had to stop the goat. His hands slipped down over the bony forehead until they covered the eyes. But still Andoar continued his frantic career. As though the obstacles he could no longer see no longer existed, he charged straight ahead. His hoofs clattered on the flat stones leading to the precipice, and the two bodies, locked together, plunged over the edge.

Robinson had witnessed the end of the struggle through his spyglass from a point two miles away. He knew that part of the island well enough to know that the shelf overgrown with brambles onto which they must have fallen could be reached either by a roundabout path from the top of the escarpment or, more directly, by climbing a hundred feet or so up the sheer rock face of which it was a part. Obviously he must take the shortest way, although the prospect of the hazardous climb terrified him. But it was not only the need to save Friday, if he were still living, that spurred him on. Though his physical aptitudes had improved enormously in recent months, he knew that among the flaws inherited from his former self was an intense fear of heights that assailed him even a few feet above the ground. He felt that in facing and overcoming this weakness he would be making a great stride in his new way of life.

Running quickly among the boulders, leaping from rock to rock the way Friday had so often done, Robinson quickly reached the point where he had to hoist himself up the smooth face of the cliff, clinging with every finger and toe to its tiny crevices. His first, but suspect, reaction was one of immense relief at finding himself in close contact with the elemental earth. His hands and feet, his whole naked body, knew the body of the mountain, its ridges and its clefts. He explored its surface with a sense of nostalgic de-light, in which concern for his physical safety played only a part. This, as he well knew, was a return to the past, which would be an act of shameful and morbid surrender were it not for the *other half* of his ordeal, the empty space at his back. There was earth and air, and between them, clinging to the rock like a trembling butterfly, was Robinson, painfully striving to effect his conversion from one to the other. Halfway up the cliff, at a place where a narrow ledge made it possible, he forced himself to pause and turn to face the emptiness. A cold sweat started on his forehead, and his hands grew dangerously slippery. He shut his eyes to avoid seeing the boulders over which he had sprung a few minutes before, which receded below him. But then he opened them again, resolved to conquer his weakness, and it occurred to him as he did so to look up at the evening sky, flooded with the last rays of the sunset. A sense of comfort instantly restored some part of his faculties. He realized that vertigo is nothing but terrestrial magnetism acting upon the spirit of man, who is the creature of earth. The soul yearns for that foothold of clay or granite, slate or silica, whose dis-tance at once terrifies and attracts, since it harbors the peace of death. It is not the emptiness of space that induces vertigo, but the enticing fullness of the earthly depths. With his face now turned to the sky, Robinson felt that something stronger than the insidious appeal of those scattered gravestones might be found in the summons to flight of two albatross, com-panionably soaring amid the pink-tinted clouds. He continued to climb, fortified in his soul and knowing better where his next steps would lead.

It was dusk when he came upon the dead body of Andoar in a clump of thorn growing on the rocky shelf. Bending over the great, shattered carcass, he saw the colored garland securely twined around its neck. A laugh sounded behind him, and there was Friday standing upright, bruised and scratched all over and with his right arm hanging limply, but otherwise unharmed.

"He died and saved me with his skin," he said. "The great goat is dead, but I shall make him fly and sing."

Friday recovered from his battering with the rapidity that always astonished Robinson. Except for his shoulder, which was bruised and wrenched but did not seem to have been broken, he was well enough next morning to return to the scene and start operations on the body of Andoar.

First he cut off the head, which he placed on an ant heap. Then, making a long incision down the chest and abdomen, and cutting around the legs, he stripped the skin from the body and spread it on the ground. He then gutted the body, removing its forty feet of intestines, and after carefully washing these in a nearby stream, draped them over the branches of a tree, a strange, bluey-white adornment which speedily attracted a multitude of flies. Then he walked singing down to the beach with Andoar's heavy, greasy pelt rolled in a bundle under his sound arm. After cleaning and soaking it thoroughly in sea water, he proceeded, using an improvised scraper made of a shell tied to a stone, to remove all the hair from one side and all traces of flesh from the other. This took him several days, during which he refused Robinson's offers of help, saying that he reserved for him a simpler and nobler task, and one that was no less important.

The nature of this task was disclosed when he asked Robinson to urinate on the skin, which was stretched out over a shallow basin in the rocks at a place where the spring tide had left a thin covering of water that evaporated in a few hours. He asked Robinson to drink a great deal during the next few days and to relieve himself nowhere else, because it was necessary for the whole skin to be soaked in urine. Robinson noted that he made no contribution of his own, but he refrained from asking whether this was because he considered his own urine to be lacking in the necessary virtues, or because he recoiled from the kind of intimacy which the mingling of their waters would have signified. After the skin had macerated for eight days in what became a brine of ammonia, Friday took it up, rinsed it in the sea, and then fixed it to a framework made of two bows held in steady tension, which served as a stretcher. Finally, he let it dry for three days in the shade, and then polished it with pumice while it still retained a trace of moisture. The skin was now a large strip of yellow parchment that sounded a full, deep note when he rubbed it with his finger.

"Andoar shall fly, Andoar shall fly," he repeated in great excitement, but without saying precisely what he intended to do.

The araucarias on the island were not numerous, but their tapered, black silhouettes rose majestically above the shrubs growing in their shade. Friday was especially fond of these trees, so common in his own country, for which they were named, and he spent entire days cradled in their branches. When he came down he would bring Robinson a handful of winged seeds containing an edible nut strongly spiced with a sharp, resinous smell. Robinson had always refused to follow him on these climbs, which he considered too reminiscent of the apes.

On this particular day, however, finding himself at the

foot of the tallest of the trees and gazing up through its branches, he calculated that it must be at least 150 feet in height. The brightness of the morning, after several days' rain, heralded the return of fine weather. The forest was steaming like an animal and the splash of invisible rivulets in the depths of its mossy undergrowth set up an unaccustomed rippling sound. Always observant of changes in himself, Robinson had noted during the past weeks that he now impatiently awaited the rising of the sun, and that the appearance of its first rays had for him the solemnity of a festival which, though it happened daily, each time brought with it a feeling of intense novelty.

Gripping the lowest branch of the araucaria, he hoisted himself onto it, first kneeling and then standing upright, with the half-formed thought that by climbing to the top he would witness the sunrise a few minutes earlier. He continued to climb, doing so without difficulty and with a growing sense of being the prisoner, and in some sort a part, of a vast and infinitely ramified structure flowing upward through the trunk with its reddish bark and spreading in countless large and lesser branches, twigs, and shoots to reach the nerve ends of leaves, triangular, pointed, scaly, and rolled in spirals around the twigs. He was taking part in the tree's most unique accomplishment, which is to embrace the air with its thousand branches, to caress it with its million fingers. As he went higher he became conscious of the swaying of the giant architectural complex through which the wind blew with the sound of an organ. He was near the top when suddenly he emerged into open space. The trunk, probably struck by lightning, was split and stripped at this point over a length of six feet. Robinson lowered his eyes in an attempt to overcome his dizziness. Beneath his feet, successive levels of branches seemed to spin away from him into terrifying depths. A nightmare of his childhood returned to him. He had resolved to climb to the top of the belfry tower of York Cathedral. After a long climb up the narrow circular stairway, built around a sculptured stone pillar, he had emerged suddenly from that protective darkness into the open sky, surrounded by space that became even more dizzying when he spied the far-off silhouette of the town's rooftops. He had had to come down wrapped up like a bundle, with his jacket pulled over his head. . . .

He shut his eyes and pressed his cheek against the trunk of the tree, his only solid support. The laboring of that living mast, with its great burden of branches carding the wind, was like a deep hum broken every now and then by a long moaning sound. He listened to this soothing music for a long time, and by degrees his terror left him. He dreamed. The tree became a great ship anchored to the earth and struggling under full sail to break away from its mooring. A warm touch fell upon his cheek and a red glow suffused his eyelids. He knew the sun had risen, but still waited a little before opening his eyes. He was absorbed in the strange new happiness rising within him, the warmth that enveloped him. After the paleness of dawn, the sun's savage light seemed to fecundate the world. He half-opened his eyes, seeing particles of brilliance dart beneath his lids. A warm breath set the leaves stirring. "The leaf is the lung of the tree which is itself a lung, and the wind is its breathing," Robinson thought. He pictured his own lungs growing outside himself like a blossoming of purple-tinted flesh, living polyparies of coral with pink membranes, sponges of human tissue. . . . He would flaunt that intricate efflorescence, that bouquet of fleshly flowers, in the wide air, while a tide of

purple ecstasy flowed into his body on a stream of crimson
blood. . . .

Across the stream a great bird shaped like a lozenge, the
color of burnished gold, was dancing in the breeze. Friday
had kept his mysterious promise to make Andoar fly.

After tying together three strips of cane to form a cross
with two parallel transverse pieces of unequal length, Friday
had cut notches at their ends, around which he twined a
length of tightly strung gut. To this light but sturdy framework he had fixed Andoar's skin, trimming it with an overlap that was folded over the gut and stitched to secure it.
The shoulders of the skin covered the upper end of the
cross, with the tail hanging from the lower end in the shape
of a clover. A loose sling ran from the ends of the central
stem, and to this the kite string was attached at a point carefully calculated to ensure that the kite would ride at the
correct angle. Friday had worked from the first flush of
dawn to put the finishing touches to his creation, while the
gusting southwesterly breeze, harbinger of fine weather,
caused the great parchment bird to jerk and quiver in his
hands, impatient for flight; and he had uttered a cry of
pleasure when, bent like a bow, his fragile creation had
soared upward from the beach with its loose parts flapping,
trailing a tail of alternating black and white feathers.
When Robinson joined him he was lying on his back on
the sand, with his hands clasped behind his neck and the kite
string tied to his left ankle. Robinson lay beside him and for
a long time they watched the flight of Andoar in the heavens
as he battled with the tricks of the wind, diving to its sudden
gusts, turning when it veered, sinking when it slackened, and

in a soaring bound regaining the altitude he had lost. Friday, participating intensely in every movement, presently got to his feet and, with arms outspread, mimicked Andoar's dance. He crouched in a huddle on the sand, then sprang in the air, flinging his left leg high; he turned and twisted, stood limply when the wind failed him, and then bounded up again; the string tied to his ankle was like a choreographic score controlling the dance, for Andoar, his faithful partner, responded to his every movement with a dip and twirl of his own.

In the afternoon they fished for sea pike in the lagoon at the eastern end of the island. Andoar, on a string about 150 feet long, was attached to the stern of the canoe, and a loose string of the same length, ending in a spray of cobweb, was tied to him, so that it hung down and brushed the crest of the waves. Robinson paddled slowly into the wind, while Friday sat with his back to him, watching the kite. When a pike rose to the bait, locking its pointed jaws of small, sharp teeth upon it, the kite dipped and jerked like an angler's float to warn them of the catch. Robinson then turned the canoe around and Friday grabbed the line when they came up to it. The canoe was presently heaped with the cylindrical, green-backed, and silver-flanked bodies of sea pike.

Friday could not bring himself to haul Andoar down that night. He tied him to one of the pepper trees between which his hammock was slung. Like a dog on the lead, Andoar passed the night at his master's feet, and he followed him about all the next day. But during the next night the wind dropped completely, and Andoar had to be retrieved from the clump of magnolias into which he had gently subsided.

After several unsuccessful efforts, Friday gave up trying to get him into the air again. He seemed to forget all about him, and spent the next week in idleness. Then, suddenly it seemed, he remembered the goat's head, which was still on the ant heap where he had left it.

The ants had done their work well. Nothing remained of flesh or skin or the long brown and white hairs of the goat's beard. The eye sockets and the inside of the skull were meticulously clean, all muscles and ligaments so thoroughly disposed of that the lower jaw fell away when Friday touched it. He held it up at arm's length as though it were a trophy, the ivory cranium with its black-ringed horns shaped like a lyre, a most noble heraldic mask. Finding the brightly colored garland which he had tied around the goat's neck, he affixed it to the horns, around the ridge which formed a bony swelling at their base.

"Andoar shall sing," he said mysteriously to Robinson, who was watching him.

First he carved two sticks of sycamore of different lengths, and, drilling a hole at either end of the longer one, he thrust it over the points of the horns so that it linked them together. The shorter stick was fixed, parallel with the first, halfway down the muzzle; and about as much above it, between the eye sockets, he fixed a bridge of pine with a dozen small notches in its outer edge. Then he brought Andoar's entrails down from the tree where they were still hanging, now dried to ribbons by the sun, and cut them into equal segments about three feet long.

Robinson, still not understanding, watched him as he might have observed the behavior of some insect whose intricate proceedings were unfathomable to the human mind. During most of his life Friday did nothing, and it seemed that boredom never intruded to ruffle the placidity of his immense and childlike indolence. But then, seized with an idea like a butterfly grub summoned by the breath of spring to engage in the complicated business of reproduction, he would jump to his feet and become wholly absorbed in activities whose purpose long remained mysterious, but which nearly always had something to do with the air and sky. When this happened neither time nor effort counted with him, and there was no limit to his perseverance or his patience. So Robinson watched while, during the next few days, Friday secured the twelve strings of gut by means of pegs to the crosspieces fixed to Andoar's horns and muzzle. He then proceeded to tune them, doing so with an instinctive musical sense, not running up the scale as with the strings of an instrument, but in unison or in octaves, so that there were no discords: for he was not devising any kind of plucking instrument, a lyre or zither, but one that was elementary, an aeolian harp, to be touched by the wind alone. The eye sockets served as sound holes bringing into play the resonance of the skull. To ensure that the harp turned to face every breath of wind, Friday attached two vulture's wings to it, causing Robinson to wonder how he had come by them, since the birds had always seemed to him invulnerable and immortal. He then hung the harp from the branch of a dead cypress standing starkly amid the waste of rock, in a place where every breeze must reach it. Indeed, no sooner was it hung than it emitted a thin, plaintive note, although the air seemed perfectly still. After listening for some minutes to this reedy lament, Friday turned to Robinson with a grimace of scorn, and raised two fingers to indicate that only two strings were sounding.

He had relapsed into his normal state of idleness, and Robinson had returned to his solar exercises, when eventually, after some weeks, Andoar gave of his best. One night Friday climbed the araucaria, where Robinson had made a nest for himself using hides for screens, and tugged at his foot. A hot, stormy wind had risen, which charged the air with electricity without bringing any promise of rain. The moon was sailing like a flung discus through thin wisps of cloud. Long before reaching the skeletal silhouette of the dead cypress, Robinson heard strains of celestial music, as though an orchestra were playing, with flutes and violins. It was not a melody to pluck at the heart with its form and rhythm, but a single note, infinite in its harmonies, which took possession of the soul, a chord composed of countless elements in whose sustained power there was something fateful and implacable that held the listener spellbound. The wind blew with increased strength as they drew near the singing tree. Tied on a short string to its topmost branch was the kite, throbbing like a drumskin, now suspended in trembling immobility, now swerving around wildly. Andoar-the-flier hovered over Andoar-the-singer, seeming both to watch over him and to threaten him. Under the shifting light of the moon the vulture's wings attached to the mask flapped wildly, lending it a fantastic semblance of life in tune with the bluster of the storm. And over all sounded that powerful, melodious song, music that was truly of the elements, inhuman music that was at once the deep voice of earth, the harmony of the spheres, and the hoarse lament of the dead goat. Huddled together in the shelter of an overhanging boulder, Robinson and Friday lost all sense of themselves in the splendor of this mystery wherein the naked elements combined—earth, tree, and wind joined in celebrating the nocturnal apotheosis of Andoar.

Not long afterward Robinson came upon the ditch where at one time he had condemned himself to penal labors for transgressing the island's laws. On these occasions he had also used it as an open-air writing room, and he found, buried in the earth, a book of notes and observations belonging to his Journal, and two unused volumes. The red ink in his small earthenware pot had long dried, and his vulture quills had disappeared. He had thought that everything was destroyed when the Residence burned. He told Friday of his discovery, and decided to continue writing the journal as a record of his progress. He thought about this for some days, and was on the point of collecting a new set of vulture's quills, and catching some more sea porcupine for the ink, when Friday brought him a bundle of carefully cut albatross quills and a pot of blue ink which he had made by crushing leaves of woad.

"Now," he said simply, "albatross is better than vulture, and blue is better than red."

CHAPTER TEN

Journal

This morning I rose before dawn, driven from my bed by a feeling of acute distress, and wandered through a world desolate in the absence of the sun, robbed of all color and relief by the uniform gray light falling from a pallid sky. I climbed to the top of the rocks, wrestling with all the strength of my spirit against the weakness of my flesh. I must take care in future not to wake until the latest possible moment before sunrise. Only sleep enables us to endure the long exile of the night, and no doubt it exists for this reason.

Suspended above the sand dunes to the east was a glow like that of a candlelit shrine in which the rites for the sun's epiphany were being mysteriously prepared. I knelt on one knee in contemplation, waiting while the nausea that had seized me was transformed into a mystical expectancy which I shared with the animals, the plants, the very stones. When I lifted my head it was as though the shrine had burst into flame, becoming a vast altar filling half the sky with its splendor of purple and gold. The first ray to start from it fell upon my red head like the protective hand of a father outstretched in benediction. The second ray purified my lips as once a burning coal had cleansed those of the prophet Isaiah. Two fiery swords then touched my shoulders and I rose to my feet, a knight of the sun. A shower of burning arrows pierced my face, breast, and hands, and the grandiose ceremony of my consecration was completed by the thousand diadems and scepters of light that bathed my more than human form.

Seated on a rock, Friday is patiently casting a line onto the ripple of the waters, fishing for gurnard. His bare feet, of which only the heels touch the rock, hang pointing downward in an extension of the line of the legs. They are like long, narrow fins, very suited to his brown, Triton body. I reflect that whereas the South American Indians have small feet and thick calves, Friday has long feet and slender calves, a characteristic of his black race. Perhaps there is always an inverse proportion between those two parts of the body. The calf muscles are triggered by the bone of the heel as by a lever. The longer the lever, the less the calf must work to flex the foot. This would explain the big calf and small foot of the yellow races, and the reverse in the case of the blacks.

O Sun, deliver me from the pull of gravity! Rid my blood of those dense humors which, though they protect me against extravagance and heedlessness, subdue the ardor of my youth and darken my joy in living. When I contemplate my somber and melancholy northern face in the mirror I realize that the two meanings of the word grace—as applied to a dancer or to a saint—may become one under this Pacific sky. Instruct me in humor. Teach me lightness of heart, the smiling acceptance of the day's gifts, without calculation or gratitude or fear.

O Sun, cause me to resemble Friday. Give me Friday's smiling countenance, his face shaped for laughter. The high forehead sweeping backward to be crowned with a garland of black curls. The eyes in which there is always a hint of derision, a touch of mockery defeated by the drollery of everything he sees. The curved, avid, and animal mouth with its uptilted corners. The backward sway of his head on his shoulders, the better to laugh, to greet with laughter everything contained in the world; and the better to reject those two vices, obtusity and malice.

But if my aeolian comrade draws me to himself, O Sun, is it not that he may guide me toward you? Sun, are you pleased with me? Look at me. Is my transformation sufficiently in the manner of your own radiance? My beard, which pointed earthward like a cluster of earthbound roots, has vanished, and now my head carries its glowing locks like a flame reaching upward to the sky.

I am an arrow aimed at your heart, a sundial proclaiming with the shadow of my erect figure your mastery of the earth, as it measures your daily progress.

I am your upright witness upon earth, a sword plunged in your flame.

❦ What has most changed in my life is the passing of time, its speed and even its direction. Formerly every day, hour, and minute leaned in a sense toward the day, hour, and minute that was to follow, and all were drawn into the pattern of the moment, whose transience created a kind of vacuum. So time passed rapidly and usefully, the more quickly because it was usefully employed, leaving behind it an accumulation of achievement and wastage which was my history. Perhaps the sweep of time of which I was a part, after winding through millennia, would have "coiled" and

returned to its beginning. But the circularity of time remained the secret of the gods, and my own short life was
no more than a segment, a straight line between two points
aimed absurdly toward infinity, like a path in a hedged garden
that tells us nothing of the curve of the earth. Yet there
are portents which offer us keys to eternity. There is the
calendar, wherein the seasons eternally complete their cycle
on a human scale, and even the modest circle of the hours.

For me the cycle has now shrunk until it is merged in the
moment. The circular movement has become so swift that it
cannot be distinguished from immobility. And it is as though,
in consequence, my days had rearranged themselves. No
longer do they jostle on each other's heels. Each stands
separate and upright, proudly affirming its own worth. And
since they are no longer to be distinguished as the stages
of a plan in process of execution, they so resemble each
other as to be superimposed in my memory, so that I seem
to be ceaselessly reliving the same day. Since the explosion
destroyed my calendar mast I have felt no need to record
the passing of time. The memory of that accident and the
events leading to it is imprinted on my mind with a vividness
which in itself reveals that time stopped when the water
clock was shattered. Are we not now living in eternity,
Friday and I?

I have still not felt all the implications of this strange
discovery. It must be noted at the outset that the revolution,
sudden and literally explosive though it was, had been heralded and perhaps anticipated by certain happenings. For
example, by my habit of stopping the water clock when I
wanted to escape from the tyrannical routine of the cultivated island. I did so at first to take refuge in its bowels,

as though escaping into timelessness. But wasn't the eternity which I looked for under the earth precisely what the explosion brought to its surface, which now sheds its benediction over all our boundaries? Or better, wasn't the explosion a volcanic release of the peace, imprisoned in the depths like a buried seed, which now prevails in the island, growing like a great tree to cast its shade farther over the land? The more I reflect upon it, the more it seems to me that the barrels of powder, Van Deyssel's pipe, and Friday's misconduct were no more than an anecdotal surface concealing a necessity that began to grow from the moment of the wreck of the Virginia.

There were also those moments of prophetic vision which, with instinctive perception, I termed my "moments of innocence." I seemed to glimpse another island hidden beneath the buildings and tilled fields which I had created on Speranza. Now I have been transported to that other Speranza, I live perpetually in a moment of innocence. Speranza is no longer a virgin land which I must make fruitful, nor Friday a savage whom I must teach to behave. Both call for all my attention, a watchful and marveling vigilance, for it seems to me—nay, I know it—that at every moment I am seeing them for the first time, and that nothing will ever dull their magical freshness.

I watch Friday as he walks toward me with his untroubled, steady pace over the shining sand of the lagoon, and the emptiness of sea and sky is so vast that I have no scale by which to measure him, so that he might be a figure three inches high within reach of my hand or a ten-foot giant half a mile away.

Here he comes. Shall I ever learn to walk with his natural

*majesty? Do I sound absurd if I say that he seems clothed
by his nakedness? He carries his body like a sovereign
affirmation, he bears himself like a monstrance of flesh. His
animal beauty proclaims itself, seeming to create a nothingness around it.*

*He leaves the lagoon and comes toward me as I sit on
the beach. But from the moment when he treads the dry
sand with its litter of broken shells, and as he passes between
a rock and a tuft of purple seaweed, becoming again a part
of our familiar landscape, his beauty wears another aspect.
It becomes grace. He smiles at me and, raising his hand in a
gesture like that of an angel in a religious painting, points
to the sky, where the southwesterly breeze is dispersing the
clouds that have accumulated during the past several days,
to restore the untrammeled reign of the sun. He skips lightly,
bringing into play a ripple of muscles. He comes up to me
but says nothing, a silent companion. He turns to look over
the lagoon he has just crossed, while his spirit seems to hover
among the mists that mark the end of an unsettled day,
leaving his body planted on the sand with its legs apart.
Seated near him, I note the part of his leg situated behind
the knee, its pearly lightness and the pattern it forms, a
capital H. It is like a throat, firm and smooth when the leg
is stretched, soft and hollow when it bends.*

*I put my hands on his knees, cupping them to fit the
shape of the knee and feel its life. In its hardness and dryness,
by contrast with the softness of the thigh, the knee is the
key to the vault on which the earthly frame is borne, raising
it aloft in a living equilibrium to the sky. There is no movement of the body, no tremor, no impulse of hesitation, that
does not proceed from that warm, moving disc and return
to it. During several seconds my hands learn that Friday's*

motionless stance is not that of a stone or tree stump, but the quivering outcome, constantly varied and readjusted, of a series of actions and reactions, the play of all his muscles.

Walking in the dusk at the edge of the marshland, I see a small animal coming toward me, reminding me at first of our poor Tenn. Then I see that it is a plump female agouti. I am downwind from it, and the little creature, which is naturally shortsighted, continues to approach without suspecting my presence. I try to turn myself into a rock or tree stump, hoping it will pass me by and go on its way. But no. Within a few yards of me it suddenly becomes rigid, ears cocked and head turned toward me with big, cloudy eyes. And then it is off like lightning, darting madly, not into the reeds, where it could vanish in an instant, but back along the path by which it came. I can still hear the scrabble of its claws on the stones when it has become no more than a bounding shadow.

I try to imagine that animal's world, dominated by the sense of smell as sight dominates the world of men. The strength and direction of the wind, so unimportant to us, are a fundamental part of it. The creature exists in the overlap between two unequally distinguishable zones. The one is the darker because the other—the zone of the wind—teems with odors. In the absence of wind the two halves of the world merge in a confused twilight, but at the least breeze the zone of wind glows with a light that turns to inky blackness when the breeze has passed. An immensely sensitive power of discrimination, comparable to the lens of the human eye, enables the scents in the windy zone to be distinguished at great distance, whether it be the scent of a particular tree, of a peccary or a parrot, or of Friday on the

*way back to his pepper trees chewing an araucaria nut—
and with the richness that is proper to the sense of smell. I
think of Tenn when Friday was digging those holes in the
ground, how he thrust his nose into the depths of the fresh-
turned soil, truly intoxicated at that moment, running and
leaping in circles around the digger and yelping with excitement and delight—so absorbed in his pursuit of smells that
for him there was nothing else.*

*As I think of it, there is nothing very astonishing in the
almost crazed intensity with which I watch Friday. What is
unbelievable is that I should have lived so long in his presence
without, so to speak, seeing him at all. How can I account
for that blind indifference, when for me he is the whole of
humanity assembled in one person, my son and my father,
my brother and my neighbor? I must concentrate every
emotion that man feels for his fellows upon this sole "other,"
because what would otherwise become of my ability to feel?
What should I do with pity and hatred, admiration and fear,
if Friday did not inspire those emotions in me? That the
fascination he holds for me is largely reciprocated has been
demonstrated several times. Two days ago he came up to
me while I lay dozing on the beach. He stood for some
moments gazing at me, a dark, slender figure outlined against
the brilliant sky. Then he knelt down beside me and began
to examine me with an extraordinary intentness. His fingers
wandered over my face, patted my cheeks, followed the
curve of my chin, tested the flexibility of my nose. He made
me raise my arms above my head, and bending over my
body he explored it inch by inch like an anatomist preparing
to dissect a corpse. He seemed to have forgotten that I lived
and breathed, that thoughts might enter my head, that I*

might grow impatient. But, understanding all too well the thirst for humankind by which he was moved, I made no attempt to stop him. In the end he smiled as though awaking from a dream and was suddenly conscious of my presence; taking my wrist, he laid his finger on a blue vein visible beneath the pale skin, and said in a tone of mock reproach, "Oh! I can see your blood!"

Am I returning to the sun cult which was a part of paganism? I think not. I know little of the beliefs and observances of those legendary "pagans," who perhaps never existed except in the imagination of our religious instructors. But it is true that, in a state of intolerable solitude that threatened to drive me to madness or suicide, I instinctively looked for some support in the absence of a social structure. The patterns of thought I had inherited from my fellow man crumbled and vanished. I groped about me, seeking salvation in communion with the elements, having myself become elemental. The earth of Speranza brought a first solution which seemed workable and lasting, although it was not without imperfections and dangers. Then Friday came, and while seeming to acquiesce in my earthly order, he did everything in his power to undermine it. But there was another way. Although the earth repelled him, Friday was as elemental by nature as I had become by force of circumstance. Under his influence, and the successive blows he dealt me, I have traveled the road of a long and painful metamorphosis. The man of earth dragged away from his element by a spirit of the air could not of himself become a creature of air. He was too dense in substance, too sluggish in his movements. But the sun with its wand of light touched the soft, white grub sunk in the shadow of the earth, and

the grub has grown into a moth with a corselet of metal, its
wings dusted with gold, a creature of the sun, hard and
impervious to the elements, but of a terrifying weakness
when the rays of the sun-god are not there to sustain it.

Andoar was myself. I myself was that solitary and stubborn old male, with his patriarch's beard and his fleece sweat-
ing lubricity, that faun of earth harshly rooted through his
four cloven hoofs to the rocky hillside. Friday conceived a
strange friendship for him, and a cruel game ensued between
them. "I will make Andoar fly and sing," Friday mysteriously
declared. But to turn the old goat into a spirit of air, what
ordeals did he inflict on his remains!

The aeolian harp. Wholly absorbed in the present, and
abhorring any task that must proceed by long, patient
stages, Friday, with an infallible instinct, chose the one instrument corresponding to his own nature. The aeolian harp
is not merely an elemental instrument drawing song from the
winds: it is also the only instrument whose music does not
need time for its development but exists entirely in the moment. You may increase the number of its strings and tune
them to whatever notes you will, but still you are composing
an instant symphony whose first and last chord sounds whenever the wind touches the harp.

I watch Friday as he dives amid the breakers rolling up
the beach; and the kind of dance in which he is engaged, the
natural grace and elegance of his movements, the gaiety, the
gleam of wet, firm flesh, all this brings to my mind the
thought of Venus rising from the waves.

This is one of the many threads of significance centered
upon Friday which I seek to disentangle, and it is related

even to the name I have bestowed on him. Friday, if I am
not mistaken, is in its ancient meaning the day of Venus. To
Christians it is the day of the death of Christ. I cannot help
feeling that in this conjunction, fortuitous though it may be,
there is a mystery beyond my grasp, and one which shocks
what is left of the devout Puritan I once was.

Another thread is contained in the last words spoken to
me before the wreck of the Virginia. Since they were in
some sort a spiritual viaticum bestowed on me by mankind
before it abandoned me to the elements, they should be imprinted on my memory in letters of fire; but the truth, alas,
is that I can recall nothing of them but a few fragments. I
mean, of course, the predictions which Captain Pieter Van
Deyssel read, or professed to read, in the tarot cards. The
name of Venus occurred several times in that utterance which
so disconcerted the young man I then was. I seem to remember the captain saying that I should become a hermit in a
cave, to be lured out of it by the coming of Venus; but
then, I fancy, this visitant from the sea changed into an
archer shooting arrows at the sun. This, however, was not
the most important part. I have a confused recollection of
a card depicting two children—twins and innocents—standing hand in hand outside a wall symbolizing the City of the
Sun. At this point Van Deyssel talked about circular sexuality
closing upon itself, and he likened it to a serpent biting its
own tail.

As to my sexuality, I may note that at no time has Friday
inspired me with any sodomite desire. For one thing, he
came too late, when my sexuality had already become elemental and was directed toward Speranza. But above all,
Venus, or Aphrodite, did not emerge from the waves and
tread my shores in order to seduce me, but to drive me

into the realm of her father, Uranus, the "sky crowned with stars," whose bleeding genitals, severed from his body and cast into the sea, broke into a white foam from which the goddess was born. It was not a matter of turning me back to human loves but, while leaving me still an elemental, of causing me to change my element. This has now happened. My love affair with Speranza was still largely human in its nature; I fecundated her soil as though I were lying with a wife. It was Friday who brought about the deeper change. The harsh stab of desire that pierces the loins of the lover has been transformed for me into a soft jubilation which exalts and pervades me from head to foot, so long as the sun-god bathes me in his rays. There is no longer that loss of substance which leaves the animal, post coitum, sad. My sky-love floods me with a vital energy which endows me with strength during an entire day and night. If this is to be translated into human language, I must consider myself feminine and the bride of the sky. But that kind of anthropomorphism is meaningless. The truth is that at the height to which Friday and I have soared, difference of sex is left behind. Friday may be identified with Venus, just as I may be said, in human terms, to open my body to the embrace of the sun.

The full moon is so bright that I can write these lines without a lamp. Friday is asleep, curled up in a ball at my feet. This atmosphere of irreality, with familiar objects lost in shadow—this starkness—gives a lightness and inconsequence to my thoughts which they atone for by the speed of their passing. This meditation will leave no trace. Ave spiritu, the thoughts that are about to die salute you! The Goddess of Fantasy hangs like a milky bubble in a sky which her own rays have swept clean of stars. Her round shape is flawless, but it is as though her substance were in turmoil, spinning as if some hidden process of creation were at work within her. Vague outlines appear and vanish on the white disc, shadowy hands reach and clasp, faces smile for an instant, to vanish into mist. The spinning gains in speed until it resembles immobility, as though the very excess of that turbulence had caused the lunar jelly to set. And gradually the pattern is defined. There are poles at either end of the egg, with a tracery of lines between them. The poles become heads, and the arabesque the outline of two conjoined bodies. Two similar beings, twins, are in process of gestation; Gemini are being born on the moon. Linked together they gently move, as though awakening after a centuries-long sleep. Their movements, which at first are like soft and drowsy caresses, suddenly change, and now they are struggling to detach themselves from one another. Each strives with his dense, obsessive shadow like a child fighting to escape from the cloying darkness of the womb. At length they separate and, ravished and solitary, reach out to rediscover their fraternal intimacy. In Leda's egg, fecundated by Jupiter, the Swan, the Dioscuri are born, Castor and Pollux, the Twins of the Sun, more intimately linked than human twins because they share a single soul. Human twins are two-souled, Gemini are one-souled. In consequence they are endowed with an unequaled density of flesh, half as much inhabited by spirit, half as porous, twice as heavy and fleshy as that of human twins. This it is that gives them their eternal youth and their inhuman beauty, the beauty of glass and metal and of shining surfaces, a glitter that does not belong to living things. They are not links in a chain running from generation to generation through the vicissitudes of history. They are the Dioscuri, beings fallen like meteors from heaven. The Sun, their father, blesses them, his flame envelops them and bestows on them the gift of eternity. . . .

A small cloud coming from the west has covered Leda's egg. Friday looks up at me with a dreaming face, mutters a few disjointed, rapid words, and then sinks back into slumber, legs drawn defensively up to his belly and fists clenched on either side of his dark head. Venus, the Swan, Leda, the Twins . . . I grope in search of myself in this forest of allegory.

CHAPTER ELEVEN

Friday was gathering blossoms of myrtle with which to make an infusion when he saw a white speck on the eastern horizon. He ran at once to tell Robinson, who was shaving. If Robinson was agitated by the news he did not show it.

"So we are going to have visitors," he said simply. "All the more reason why I should complete my toilet."

In a state of high excitement Friday climbed to the top of the rocks, taking with him the spyglass. The ship was a topsail schooner under a full head of sail, heading at a speed of perhaps a dozen knots in the stiff, southwesterly breeze for the marshy side of the island. Friday ran back to report this to Robinson, who was now putting the finishing touches to his sun-bleached locks with a tortoise-shell comb, and then returned to his observation post. The vessel had gone over to the starboard tack, evidently because her captain realized that this side of the island was not suitable for landing, and under shortened sail was proceeding on a course parallel with the coast. Friday hurried to tell Robinson that she was passing the sand dunes and would presumably bring up in the Bay of Salvation. The first thing was to ascertain her nationality. Together they ran to the edge of the trees bordering the beach, and Robinson studied her through the spyglass. She was now turning into the wind two cable lengths offshore; her sails were coming down and they heard the rattle of the anchor chain.

She was a vessel of a kind unfamiliar to Robinson, evidently of recent design, but she was flying the colors of His Britannic Majesty. Accordingly Robinson emerged from his concealment and walked onto the beach with the composure proper to a monarch welcoming visitors to his realm. He watched while a longboat was lowered in a splash of spray and a party of men headed for the shore.

As he stood gazing at the sweep of the oars, Robinson was suddenly conscious of the enormous weight of the few moments that remained before the man in the bow staved off the first rocks with his boat hook. He had a vision, like that of a drowning man, of his whole life on the island— the building of the *Escape*, the mire, the frenetic cultivation of Speranza, the cave, the coomb, the coming of Friday, the explosion—above all, the measureless extent of time during which his conversion to the sun had been completed in tranquil happiness.

There were a number of casks in the boat, which was evidently coming ashore for water, and, standing in the stern sheets, top-booted and armed, was a black-bearded man wearing a straw hat. He was the forerunner of the community of mankind which was now to enmesh Robinson in the tangle of its words and deeds, and restore him to the great complex of civilization. The world so patiently woven and elaborated during the long years of solitude would be tested to the uttermost when Robinson's hand clasped that of this envoy of humanity.

There was a grating sound as the boat grounded, and the sailors jumped out and pulled her up onto the beach, out of reach of the rising tide. The bearded man held out his hand to Robinson.

"William Hunter, captain of the schooner *Whitebird*, from Blackpool."

"What is the date?" asked Robinson.

The captain turned in surprise to the man standing beside him, who seemed to be the mate.

"What's the date, Joe?"

"December 22, sir."

"But the year?" demanded Robinson. "The year?"

"Why, it's 1787."

Robinson made a rapid calculation. The *Virginia* had been wrecked on September 30, 1759—that was to say, twenty-eight years, two months, and some twenty days ago. Despite all the things that had happened, and the extent of the change in himself, he found this vast span of time almost unbelievable. He could not venture to ask if they were sure of the year, which to him was like a date in the still distant future. Indeed, he decided instantly not to tell them the date of the wreck of the *Virginia*, out of a kind of apprehension, a fear that they would not believe him, or would think of him as a freakish apparition.

"I was cast ashore on this island by the wreck of the brig *Virginia*, commanded by Captain Pieter Van Deyssel of Flushing," he said. "I was the only survivor. The shock has played tricks with my memory, and I cannot remember what year it was."

"I don't recall the loss of a vessel of that name," said Hunter. "But the war with America has greatly affected maritime relations."

Robinson knew nothing of this war. He saw that he would

need to exercise great prudence if he was to conceal his ignorance of what had been happening in the world.

Friday meanwhile, after helping the boat's crew to unload their casks, was guiding them to the nearest stream. Robinson was struck by his ease in getting along with this party of foreigners, while he himself felt so remote from their captain. Evidently Friday was ingratiating himself with them because he hoped to be taken on board the *Whitebird;* nor could Robinson deny that he, too, was eager to visit the fine, fore-and-aft-rigged vessel with her low, raking lines, so clearly built for speed. But at the same time, these men and the world they brought with them caused him an overwhelming discomfort which he was struggling to overcome. He was still alive. He had triumphed over madness during his years of solitude. He had achieved a state of stability, or series of states, in which he and Speranza, and then Speranza, Friday, and himself had formed a unity which endured and had brought supreme happiness. After much suffering and many fateful crises he now felt able, with Friday at his side, to defy the passage of time and, like a meteor launched frictionless in space, to continue indefinitely on his course without weariness or loss of momentum. Nevertheless, a confrontation with other men was a supreme test that might enable him to accomplish even more. It might be that, returning to England, he would manage not only to preserve the solar happiness he had attained, but to increase its intensity in the city of men. Thus had Zoroaster, after forging his soul in the heat of the desert sun, returned to the corrupt turmoil of mankind to dispense his wisdom.

Meanwhile, he was laboriously engaged with Hunter in a conversation which threatened to lapse into uneasy silence. He had volunteered to show him what the island had to offer in the way of game, fresh fruits, and vegetables as a protection against scurvy, and two of the sailors were already climbing coconut palms to cut down nuts, while others could be heard shouting as they hunted the goats. Robinson reflected, not without pride, on the acute distress it would have caused him in the days of the cultivated island to see it pillaged in this fashion. It was not so much the senseless mutilation of the trees or the heedless slaughter of the animals that now troubled him, but the coarse and avaricious bearing of these men who were his fellows, so familiar to him and yet so strange. The place where Speranza's counting-house had once stood was now overgrown with tall grass that swayed with a silken rustle in the wind; and here one of the sailors had discovered two pieces of gold. He shouted to his comrades, and after an excited dispute they resolved to set fire to the grass in the hope of finding more. The fact that the gold in a sense belonged to him scarcely occurred to Robinson, nor did he give much thought to the animals who were to be deprived of the only pasture which the rainy season did not turn into a swamp. He was too absorbed in listening to the quarrels that broke out with each new discovery, and he paid little attention to the captain, who was telling him how during the war he had sunk a French troopship carrying reinforcements to the American rebels. The mate, on Robinson's other side, was talking about the slave trade and the huge profits to be derived from it. Both men were absorbed in their own preoccupations, and neither thought of questioning him about his life on the island. Even the presence of Friday did not seem to interest them. And Robinson knew that in former times he had been as they were, driven by the same motives of greed, arrogance, and violence, and that a part of him was still at one with them. Thinking this, he continued to observe them with the detachment of a naturalist studying a colony of bees or ants, or the dubious forms of life that are to be found under a stone.

Each of these men was a *possible* world, having its own coherence, its values, its sources of attraction and repulsion, its center of gravity. And with all the differences between them, each of these possible worlds at that moment shared a vision, casual and superficial, of the island of Speranza, which caused them to act in common, and which incidentally contained a shipwrecked man called Robinson and his half-caste servant. For the present this picture occupied their minds, but for each of them it was purely temporary, destined very soon to be returned to the limbo from which it had been briefly plucked by the accident of the *Whitebird*'s getting off course. And each of these possible worlds naïvely proclaimed itself the reality. That was what other people were: the possible obstinately passing for the real. All Robinson's upbringing had taught him that to reject their affirmation was cruel, egotistical, and immoral; but this was an attitude of mind that he had lost during the years, and now he wondered if he could ever recover it. Mingled with the claims of those possible worlds to exist was their picture of a Speranza doomed to disappear, and it seemed to him that in granting them reality he was vowing Speranza to destruction.

The boat had gone off to the schooner, loaded to the gunwales with fruit, game, vegetables, and a few living but hamstrung goats. It now returned, and the crew stood by awaiting orders.

"You will of course do me the honor of dining with me," the captain said; and without waiting for Robinson's reply he instructed the men to take the fresh water to the ship and then come back to get them. Being left alone with Robinson, he shed something of the reserve he had maintained since landing and talked, not without bitterness, of his life during the past four years.

As a youthful and enthusiastic naval officer he had fought under Admiral Howe in the War of American Independence and had distinguished himself at the battle of Brooklyn and the capture of New York; but he had been quite unprepared for the reverses that had followed those early successes.

"Young Service officers are taught to think in terms of nothing but victory," he said. "It would be wiser to teach them to recover from defeat. To be routed and regroup one's forces, or to be forced to break off a sea action with spars and rigging shot to pieces, and carry out repairs at sea and turn back to re-engage the enemy—that's the hardest thing to learn. But it is an art that our leaders consider shameful to teach us, although we learn from the history books that many great victories have sprung from defeat, and every stableboy knows that the horse that leads at the start of the race is most likely to be beaten at the post."

The British defeat at Saratoga, which had brought France into the war on the side of the colonists, and France's sea victories off Grenada and Tobago had inspired Hunter with a permanent hatred of the French; and the shame of the eventual British capitulation, the surrender of what was then the brightest jewel in the English crown, had caused him to resign his commission.

For a time he had sailed a merchant ship, but the prosaic squalor of this life, the greed of shipowners, the bills of lading, the handling of cargoes that were often suspect, the bickering with customs and excise men—none of this had suited him. When he was on the verge of giving up the sea altogether a stroke of luck had befallen him—the only one, he added, in his life. He had been offered the command of the *Whitebird*, whose light build and speedy lines made her especially suitable for less bulky cargoes—tea, spices, rare metals, precious stones, and opium—a trade entailing long voyages, with a touch of mystery and adventure that appealed to his romantic nature. Perhaps he might have been happier still as a buccaneer or freebooter, but his naval training had left him with an instinctive aversion for activities of a disreputable nature.

When Robinson jumped down onto the deck of the *Whitebird* he was greeted by a radiant Friday who had been brought on board with the boat's previous trip. He had evidently been made the pet of the ship's company, and he seemed as much at home as if he had spent his entire life on her. Robinson had had occasion to note in the past that the only artifacts which impressed primitive peoples were things coming within their scope, such as knives, clothes, small boats. Beyond this they were unmoved, as though a mansion or rigged ship were a work of nature, no more to be marveled at than a cavern or an iceberg. It was not so with Friday, and Robinson at first assumed that the Araucanian's ready understanding of everything he saw was due to his own influence. But as he watched him run up the shrouds and stand laughing on the crosstrees, fifty feet above deck, he thought of Friday's airy contrivances—the arrows, the kite, and the harp—and realized that for him this sailing ship, so graceful and handsomely rigged, represented a supreme conquest of the air. The thought saddened him, the more so since he was conscious of his own growing revulsion for this world, into which he was being dragged, it seemed to him, against his will.

His unhappiness increased at the sight of a small, half-naked figure crouched at the foot of one of the masts, to which it was tied. It was a boy of about twelve, lean as a skinned cat. His face was hidden. A thick mass of red hair made his narrow shoulders with their sharp shoulder blades seem even more brittle, and there was a series of broad welts, some bleeding slightly, across his back.

"That's Jaan, the galley boy," Hunter said. He turned and asked: "What's he been doing now?"

In answer to the question a round, red face, that of the ship's cook, shot up through the galley hatch like a jack-in-the-box.

"He spoiled the pasty I was making by salting it three times over," the cook growled. "He never thinks what he's doing. I've given him a touch of the rope's end and he'll get more if he doesn't mend his ways."

"Better untie him," the captain said. "We shall want him to wait at table."

Robinson dined in the captain's cabin with Hunter and the first mate. He did not see what became of Friday, who was presumably eating with the crew. Sustaining the conversation was not difficult. His hosts seemed to have made up their minds that he had everything to learn and nothing of consequence to tell them about Friday or himself, and the convenient assumption enabled him to observe and reflect at leisure. It was of course true, in a sense, that he had everything to learn, or rather to assimilate and digest; but what he heard was to him as heavy and indigestible as the food on his plate, and he was afraid that a sudden attack of nausea might cause him to vomit not only this but the whole world he was encountering.

What principally repelled him was not so much the coarse brutality, the greed and animosity that emerged so clearly from the discourse of these two civilized and perfectly honorable men. It was easy to imagine encountering men of a different stamp, mild-mannered, benevolent, and generous. For Robinson the evil went deeper, and he defined it to himself as the incurable pettiness of the ends to which all men feverishly devoted their lives. Each was in search of something, some special acquisition, wealth or personal satisfaction; but why that thing more than another? None could have told him. He imagined himself asking Hunter, for example, "What do you live for?" Hunter would have had no reply, and no recourse but to ask the question in return; and Robinson would have answered it by pointing one hand to the shores of Speranza and with the other to the sun. After a moment of stupefaction Hunter would have burst out laughing, the laughter of folly in the face of wisdom: for what was the sun to him but a gigantic flame? How could he conceive of it as possessing a spirit that could irradiate with eternity those who had learned to open their hearts to it?

The boy, Jaan, was waiting on them, half-hidden behind a large, white apron. His small, bony, freckled face looked smaller still under the tangled mop of hair, and Robinson tried to meet his eyes, which were so blue that it was as though the sky were shining through his head. But he paid little attention to the visitor, being too terrified of making some blunder as he served them. Hunter had the habit, after speaking a few words with a sort of controlled vehemence, of lapsing into a moody or disdainful silence, like the garrison of a besieged fortress, which after damaging the enemy with a sudden sortie returns hastily to the shelter of its walls. The gaps were filled by the discourse of the mate, Joseph, who, entirely concerned with practical matters and the newest developments in the art of navigation, evidently felt for his commander a warm esteem sustained by a total lack of comprehension. It was he who, when the meal was over, took Robinson on deck, leaving the captain below. He was particularly anxious to show him the ship's sextant, a novel appliance whereby the altitude of the sun could be observed, and latitude and longitude determined, with an accuracy incomparably greater than that of the old quadrant method. Robinson was interested by the enthusiastic lecture and it gave him pleasure to handle the gleaming brass and ivory instrument, but what principally struck him was the display of liveliness in a mind that was otherwise so circumscribed. Intelligence and stupidity could live together in the same head, mixing no more than oil and water. When he was talking of index and horizon glasses, of the vernier scale, and angles of incidence, Joseph glowed with intelligence; but only a few minutes before he had been saying of the boy, Jaan, that he had no call to complain of a whipping, because his mother was nothing but a dockside whore.

The sun was beginning to set. It was the hour when Robinson was accustomed to bathe in its rays in order to store himself with energy and warmth before the shadows lengthened and the evening breeze caused the eucalyptus trees along the beach to whisper among themselves. At Joseph's suggestion he stretched himself on the poop deck and lay for a long time watching the truck of the topmast as it described invisible patterns in a deep blue sky, where a slender crescent moon hung like a shred of transparent porcelain. He turned his head to look at Speranza, the pale line of sand at the water's edge and the rising flow of greenery leading to the jagged rock beyond. Then it was that he bowed to the decision that all day had been forming within him, the inexorable resolve to let the *Whitebird* sail without him, and to remain on the island with Friday. Even more than by the gulf that separated him from the men aboard that ship, he felt pushed to this decision by his panic rejection of the degrading and mortal turbulence of the times in which they lived, and which they spread around them. December 22, 1787. Twenty-eight years, two months, and some twenty days. The figure still amazed him. If he had not been cast ashore on Speranza he would now be in his fifties, a graybeard with creaking bones. His children would be older than he had been when he left them, and perhaps he would be a grandfather. But none of these things had happened to him. Speranza lay only two cables distant from the ship and the miasma that pervaded it, a glowing denial of that sinister degradation. The truth was that he was younger today than the pious and self-seeking young man who had set sail in the *Virginia*, not young with a biological youth, corruptible and harboring the seeds of its decrepitude, but with a mineral youth, solar and divine. Every day was for him a first beginning, an absolute beginning of the history of the world. Beneath the rays of the sun-god, Speranza trembled in an eternal present, without past or future. He could not forsake that eternal instant, poised at the needle point of ecstasy, to sink back into a world of usury, dust, and decay.

When he announced his intention of staying on the island, only Joseph seemed surprised. Hunter merely smiled coldly. Perhaps he was relieved at not having to burden himself with two passengers in a ship where there was little room to spare. He had the courtesy to treat the supplies he had brought on board as though they had been the property of Robinson, the master of the island, and he offered him in exchange a gig which he carried lashed on the poop deck, and which was additional to the ship's normal complement of boats. It was a handy little craft, more seaworthy than Robinson's aged canoe, and he and Friday rowed themselves ashore in it as darkness fell.

Robinson's joy at repossessing the realm which he had believed lost to him forever was reflected in the last red glow of the sunset. Immense though his comfort was, there was a hint of funereal solemnity in the peace that surrounded him. He felt not hurt, but aged, as though his visit to the *Whitebird* had marked the end of a very long and happy youth. Yet what did this matter? The English ship would weigh anchor by the first light of dawn, and resume her wandering course guided by the whim of her shadowy commander. The waters of the Bay of Salvation would close behind the wake of the only vessel that had entered them in twenty-eight years. Robinson had let it be known that he would prefer the whereabouts of the island not to be revealed, and the wish was too much in accordance with Hunter's own strange character for him not to respect it. Thus the matter would be closed, terminating the daylong interlude that had brought tumult and upheaval into the Twins' serene eternity.

CHAPTER TWELVE

It was still pale dawn when Robinson climbed down from his nest in the araucaria. He had formed the habit of sleeping until the last minutes before sunrise, to reduce as much as possible that mournful period of waiting, the most lifeless of the whole day, because the furthest removed from sunset. But the unaccustomed food, the wine, and a deep-seated unease in himself had made his slumber feverish, with sudden starts and periods of unfruitful wakefulness. Lying in darkness, he had been the defenseless prey of old thoughts and tormenting obsessions. He rose early to escape the turmoil in his mind.

He walked on to the beach. As he had expected, the *Whitebird* was gone. The sea was gray under a colorless sky, and a heavy dew weighted the plants with a pale luminosity that was neither light nor shade, but mercilessly clear. Even the birds were silent. Robinson felt a hollow of despair growing in him, a black, resounding emptiness like a spirit of evil that filled his heart with sickness and his mouth with a bitter juice. A wave ran sluggishly up the beach, toyed for an instant with the body of a dead crab, and then withdrew as though in disappointment. In a little while, an hour at the most, the sun would shine, restoring life and joy to all things, and to Robinson. He must hold out until then, and resist the temptation to awaken Friday.

There could be no doubt that the coming of the *White-bird* had seriously disturbed the delicate balance of the trio they formed, Robinson, Friday, and Speranza. Speranza's wounds were but superficial and would vanish in a few months; but how long would it take Friday to forget the swift, graceful ship so tender to every touch of the wind? Robinson now reproached himself for having decided to remain on the island without first discussing the matter with Friday. Well, today he would tell him what he had learned from Joseph of the horrors of the slave trade and the life that awaited the blacks in the plantations of the New World. His regrets, if he had any, would thereby be lessened.

Thinking of this, he walked automatically toward the two pepper trees between which Friday's hammock was slung. He did not mean to wake him but only to watch him as he slept, to draw comfort from the innocent tranquillity of his presence.

The hammock was empty. What was more surprising was the absence of the trifles with which Friday amused himself during his siestas—a mirror, his blowpipe, a reed pipe, a handful of feathers, and so on. Robinson ran down to the beach again. The gig and the canoe were both there, drawn up on the shore. But surely if Friday had gone back to the *Whitebird*, he would have taken one of them.

Robinson began to scour the whole island, calling Friday's name. Running, stumbling, and shouting, he dashed from the Bay of Salvation to the eastern sand dunes, from the cave to the pink coomb, from the woodlands on the western side to the lagoon, with the growing, despairing conviction that this was all in vain. He did not understand Friday's desertion, but he could not escape the conclusion that he was alone on the island, as alone as he had been at the beginning. The frantic search completed his demoralization by taking him to places, full of memories, that he had not visited for months. He felt the crumbling remains of the *Escape* under his hands, and the tepid warmth of the mire beneath his feet. He found in the forest a part of the charred leather binding of his Bible. All the pages had been burned, except for a fragment containing the first lines of the Book of Kings; and in a weak daze he read:

"Now King David was old and stricken in years; and they covered him with clothes, but he gat no heat."

"Wherefore his servants said unto him, Let there be sought for my lord the King a young virgin: and let her stand before the King, and let her cherish him, and let her lie in thy bosom, that my lord the King may get heat."

Robinson perceived that the twenty-eight years, which until yesterday did not exist, had now closed down upon him. The *Whitebird* had brought them with her like the germs of a mortal disease, and suddenly he was an old man. He realized also that for an old man there is no greater affliction than solitude. *"Let her lie in thy bosom, that my lord the King may get heat."* Indeed, he was shivering with cold in the dew of the morning, and never again would there be anyone to warm him. He came upon a last relic, Tenn's collar, moldy with damp. All the years that had seemed effaced were suddenly recalled with these prosaic and heart-rending vestiges. He pressed his forehead against the trunk of a cypress and his lips quivered, but old men do not weep. His stomach heaved and he vomited the winy remains of the meal he had eaten on board the ship. When he looked up he found himself surrounded by a circle of vultures, standing only a few yards distant and gazing at him with pink eyes. They too had come to keep this appointment with the past.

Was he now to begin all over again—the tilled fields, the breeding pens, the buildings—while he awaited the coming of another Friday who would sweep it all away in a burst of flame and raise him again to the heights? A mockery! The truth was that now his only choice was between time and eternity. Eternal rebirth, that bastard offspring of both, was only a form of madness. There was only one way of salvation: he must seek to regain that timeless limbo, peopled by innocents, which he had gradually attained and from which the visit of the *Whitebird* had caused him to fall. But how, being old and without strength, could he hope to recover that state of grace that was so slow and difficult of achievement? How could it happen, except simply by the act of dying? Wasn't this the only eternity that remained to him, death in this island where perhaps for decades no other person would set foot? But he must outwit the vultures, who seemed to be mysteriously aware of what was taking place, and waited to perform their funeral office. His bones must whiten beneath the stones of Speranza like spillikins whose assemblage no one must disturb. That would be a fitting end to the strange and unsung tale of the solitary of Speranza.

He made his way slowly to the mound of rock which had buried the mouth of the cave, feeling sure that by wriggling between the boulders he could bury himself deeply enough to escape any animal visitation. Perhaps by the exercise of extreme patience he might even penetrate into the cave itself and down to that lowest recess. There he need only huddle like a fetus and close his eyes for life to slip away from him, so utter was his weariness, so deep his despair.

He found a crevice scarcely larger than a rabbit's burrow but which, in his diminished state, he felt he could crawl through. He was examining it to see how far it went when he thought he detected a movement. A pebble rattled in its depths, and in the mouth of the crevice a body appeared. After some wriggling it emerged, and a child stood before Robinson with one arm shielding his face—against the daylight or against a blow. Robinson stepped back, dumbfounded.

"Who are you?" he asked. "What are you doing here?"

"I was the cook's boy aboard the *Whitebird*," the child replied. "I was unhappy. I saw you look at me when I was waiting at table, and your eyes were kind. When I heard that you were not going to sail with us I decided to escape to this island to be with you. Last night, when I was about to lower myself over the side and swim ashore, I saw a man come aboard from a canoe. It was your native servant. He cast the canoe adrift and went straight to the mate's cabin, where the mate seemed to be expecting him. So then I guessed that he intended to stay on board. I swam to the canoe and paddled to the island. I have been hiding here ever since. And," the child concluded on a note of triumph, "the *Whitebird* has sailed without me."

"Come with me," said Robinson.

He took the boy by the hand, and together they began to climb the slope leading to the sharp peak of rock which was the highest point of the island. Halfway up Robinson stopped and turned to look at the boy. The light blue eyes with pale albino lashes gazed up at him, and the boy smiled faintly. Robinson opened his hand to examine the hand it was clasping, and was touched to see it so slender and frail, yet callused by the rough work of the ship.

"I'm going to show you something," he said in the effort to control his emotions, without quite knowing what he meant.

The island at their feet was partly shrouded in mist, but a glow had begun to appear within the gray of the eastern sky. The gig and the canoe were beginning to stir slightly as the rising tide lapped around them. To the north a gleam of white was speeding toward the horizon, and Robinson pointed toward it.

"Look well at it," he said. "A ship within sight of Speranza. It is something you may never see again."

The gleam grew smaller and was presently lost in the distance, and it was at this moment that the sun loosed its first arrows. A cricket chirped. A gull swooped down to the mirror surface of the sea, and a moment later soared upward with broad wings flapping and a silver fish in its beak. The sky in an instant had become pale blue. The flowers which had hung with their closed petals bowing to the west now turned and spread them wide toward the east, and the song of birds and insects rose in the air. Robinson had forgotten the boy. Drawn up to his full height, he was confronting the solar ecstasy with a joy that was almost painful, while the bright splendor in which he bathed washed him clean of the grime of the past day and night. A blade of fire seemed to penetrate his flesh, causing his whole being to tremble. Speranza was shedding her veil of mist, to emerge unsullied and intact. Indeed, it was as though the agony and the nightmare had never taken place. Eternity, reasserting its hold on him, had effaced that ugly but trivial interlude. He drew a deep breath, filled with a sense of utter contentment, and his chest swelled like a breastplate of brass. His feet were solidly planted on the rock, and his legs sturdy and unshakable as columns of stone. The glowing light clad him in an armor of unfading youth and set upon his head a helmet flawlessly polished and a visor with diamond eyes. At length the sun-god unfolded his whole rich crown of flaming hair with a clash of cymbals and a fanfare of trumpets; and gleams of gold shone on the boy's head.

"What is your name?" asked Robinson.

"I am called Jaan Neljapäev. I was born in Estonia," the boy replied, seeming to apologize for the difficult name.

"I shall call you Sunday," said Robinson. "It is the day of the resurrection, of the youth of all things, and the day of our master, the Sun." He added, smiling: "To me you will always be Sunday's child."

Born in Paris in 1924, Michel Tournier has unusually close ties to Germany: both his parents were German scholars, and he studied at the University of Tübingen. He holds master's degrees in both law and philosophy, and worked for some years at a large French publishing house. He is fascinated by photography, and has produced his own programs for French television. His first novel, *Friday*, won the Grand Prix du Roman of the Académie Française. His second, *The Ogre*, is the only novel ever to win France's most prestigious literary prize, the Prix Goncourt, by a unanimous vote. Like his two subsequent novels, *Gemini* and *The Four Wise Men*, and his recently published short story collection, *The Fetishist*, they received enthusiastic reviews around the world.

A bachelor, Michel Tournier lives near Paris, and devotes most of his time to writing.

PANTHEON MODERN WRITERS SERIES

BLOW-UP AND OTHER STORIES
by Julio Cortázar, translated by Paul Blackburn

A celebrated masterpiece: fifteen eerie and brilliant short stories by the great Latin American writer.

"A splendid collection."—*The New Yorker*

"Cortázar at his best."—Michael Wood

"Maddeningly unforgettable."—*Saturday Review*
0-394-72881-5 $6.95

THE WINNERS
by Julio Cortázar, translated by Elaine Kerrigan

Julio Cortázar's superb first novel about life—and death—on a South American luxury cruise.

"This formidable novel...introduces a dazzling writer....[*The Winners*] is irresistibly readable."—*The New York Times Book Review*
0-394-72301-5 $8.95

THE OGRE
by Michel Tournier, translated by Barbara Bray

The story of a gentle giant's extraordinary experiences in World War II—a gripping tale of innocence, perversion, and obsession.

"The most important novel to come out of France since Proust."—Janet Flanner

"Quite simply, a great novel."—*The New Yorker*
0-394-72407-0 $8.95

FRIDAY
by Michel Tournier, translated by Norman Denny

A sly, enchanting retelling of the story of Robinson Crusoe, in which Friday teaches Crusoe that there are better things in life than civilization.

"A literary pleasure not to miss."—Janet Flanner

"A fascinating, unusual novel...a remarkably heady French wine in the old English bottle."—*The New York Times Book Review*
0-394-72880-7 $7.95

THE WALL JUMPER
by Peter Schneider, translated by Leigh Hafrey

A powerful, witty novel of life in modern Berlin.

"Marvelous...creates, in very few words, the unreal reality of Berlin."—Salman Rushdie, *The New York Times Book Review*

"A document of our time, in which fiction has the force of an eyewitness account."—*The* [London] *Times Literary Supplement*
0-394-72882-3 $6.95

PANTHEON MODERN WRITERS SERIES

ADIEUX: A FAREWELL TO SARTRE
by Simone de Beauvoir, translated by Patrick O'Brian

Simone de Beauvoir's moving farewell to Jean-Paul Sartre, her lifelong companion, in two parts: an account of his last ten years and an interview with him about his life and work.

"An intimate, personal, and honest portrait of a relationship unlike any other in literary history."—Deirdre Bair

0-394-72898-X   **$8.95**

A VERY EASY DEATH
by Simone de Beauvoir, translated by Patrick O'Brian

The profoundly moving, day-by-day account of the death of the author's mother, at once intimate and universal.

"A beautiful book, sincere and sensitive."—Pierre-Henri Simon

0-394-72899-8   **$4.95**

WHEN THINGS OF THE SPIRIT COME FIRST:
FIVE EARLY TALES
by Simone de Beauvoir, translated by Patrick O'Brian

The first paperback edition of the marvelous early fiction of Simone de Beauvoir.

"An event for celebration."—*The New York Times Book Review*

0-394-72235-3   **$5.95**

THE BLOOD OF OTHERS
by Simone de Beauvoir, translated by Roger Senhouse and Yvonne Moyse

A brilliant existentialist novel about the French resistance.

"A novel with a remarkably sustained note of suspense and mounting excitement due to the sheer vitality and force of de Beauvoir's ideas."—*Saturday Review*

0-394-72411-9   **$6.95**

NAPLES '44
by Norman Lewis

A young British intelligence officer's powerful journal of his year in Allied-occupied Naples.

"An immensely gripping experience...a marvelous book...his compassion and humor are just plain terrific."—S. J. Perelman

0-394-72300-7   **$7.95**

PANTHEON MODERN CLASSICS

MEMED MY HAWK
by Yashar Kemal, translated by Eduardo Roditi

The most important novel to come out of modern Turkey, this vital and exciting story of a latter-day Robin Hood is set against the beauty and brutality of Turkish peasant life.

"Exciting, rushing, lyrical, a complete and subtle emotional experience."—*The Chicago Sun-Times*

0-394-71016-9 $6.95

THE LEOPARD
by Giuseppe di Lampedusa, translated by Archibald Colquhoun

This powerful novel of a Sicilian prince perched on the brink of great historic change is widely acknowledged as a masterpiece of European literature.

"The finest historical novel I have read in years."—*Saturday Review*
0-394-74949-9 $5.95

YOUNG TÖRLESS
by Robert Musil, translated by Eithne Williams and Ernst Kaiser

Taut, compelling, pitiless first novel by the author of *The Man Without Qualities*. A meticulous account, set in an Austrian military academy, of the discovery and abuse of power—physical, emotional, and sexual.

"An illumination of the dark places of the heart everywhere."—*The Washington Post*

0-394-71015-0 $5.95

THE STORY OF A LIFE
by Konstantin Paustovsky, translated by Joseph Barnes

Universally acclaimed memoir of Russian boyhood coming of age amidst war and revolution. A startlingly vivid, deeply personal yet panoramic view of Russia during the tumultuous first two decades of the twentieth century.

"A work of astonishing beauty...a masterpiece."—Isaac Bashevis Singer
0-394-71014-2 $8.95